IS IT TRUE WHAT THE HATEMONGERS SAY ABOUT ELVIS?

No, it isn't true about the drugs that supposedly left him a grotesque caricature of a human being.

It isn't true about the orgies at his fabulous mansion, Graceland, and about his rumored sexual appetites and tastes.

It isn't true about his rages, his arrogance, his near-madness.

What *is* true is that after Elvis Presley's death, scandalmongers gathered like vultures to feed off his fame. Now, at last, May Mann, the woman who knew him so intimately right up to his agonizing end, brings Elvis and his last years back to life—and back to the hearts of all who fell under his spell as a giant of an entertainer and a giant of a man.

ELVIS, WHY WON'T THEY LEAVE YOU ALONE?

More Biography and Autobiography from SIGNET

(0451)

- ☐ **BOB DYLAN by Anthony Scaduto with an introduction by Steven Gaines.** (092899—$2.50)*
- ☐ **UP & DOWN WITH THE ROLLING STONES by Tony Sanchez.** (120302—$3.50)
- ☐ **SINATRA by Earl Wilson.** (074874—$2.25)
- ☐ **FONDA: MY LIFE as told to Howard Teichmann.** (118588—$3.95)*
- ☐ **ALAN ALDA: AN UNAUTHORIZED BIOGRAPHY by Jason Bonderoff.** (119339—$2.95)
- ☐ **BOGIE by Joe Hyams.** (091892—$1.75)
- ☐ **KATE: THE LIFE OF KATHERINE HEPBURN by Charles Higham.** (112121—$2.95)*
- ☐ **MARILYN: AN UNTOLD STORY by Norman Rosten.** (088808—$1.50)
- ☐ **RICHARD DAWSON AND FAMILY FEUD by Mary Ann Norborn.** (097734—$1.95)*
- ☐ **STEVE MARTIN—AN UNAUTHORIZED *BIOGRAPHY* WELL EXCUUUSE US by Marsha Daly.** (092066—$2.25)
- ☐ **STEVE MCQUEEN—THE UNAUTHORIZED BIOGRAPHY by Malachy McCoy.** (099303—$2.50)
- ☐ **FIRST, YOU CRY by Betty Rollin.** (112598—$2.50)
- ☐ **IF YOU COULD SEE WHAT I HEAR by Tom Sullivan and Derek Gill.** (118111—$2.75)*

*Prices slightly higher in Canada

Buy them at your local bookstore or use this convenient coupon for ordering.
THE NEW AMERICAN LIBRARY, INC.,
P.O. Box 999, Bergenfield, New Jersey 07621
Please send me the books I have checked above. I am enclosing $_____
(please add $1.00 to this order to cover postage and handling). Send check or money order—no cash or C.O.D.'s. Prices and numbers are subject to change without notice.
Name_____
Address_____
City _____ State _____ Zip Code _____
Allow 4-6 weeks for delivery.
This offer is subject to withdrawal without notice.

ELVIS
WHY WON'T THEY LEAVE YOU ALONE?

MAY MANN

A SIGNET BOOK
NEW AMERICAN LIBRARY
TIMES MIRROR

NAL BOOKS ARE AVAILABLE AT QUANTITY DISCOUNTS
WHEN USED TO PROMOTE PRODUCTS OR SERVICES. FOR
INFORMATION PLEASE WRITE TO PREMIUM MARKETING DIVISION,
THE NEW AMERICAN LIBRARY, INC., 1633 BROADWAY,
NEW YORK, NEW YORK 10019.

Copyright © 1982 by May Mann

All rights reserved

SIGNET TRADEMARK REG. U.S. PAT. OFF. AND FOREIGN COUNTRIES
REGISTERED TRADEMARK—MARCA REGISTRADA
HECHO EN CHICAGO, U.S.A.

SIGNET, SIGNET CLASSICS, MENTOR, PLUME, MERIDIAN AND NAL BOOKS
are published by The New American Library, Inc.,
1633 Broadway, New York, New York 10019

First Printing, November, 1982

1 2 3 4 5 6 7 8 9

PRINTED IN THE UNITED STATES OF AMERICA

Respectfully, I dedicate this book to Lisa Marie Presley, and to my father, Oscar Perry Randall, who was so much like Elvis . . . a handsome, talented charmer, a self-made millionaire, a look-alike for Tyrone Power . . . who lived a full, glorious life, and died at age thirty-four . . . leaving me, his only child, always longing for "my daddy." I well know Lisa Marie's loneliness for hers . . . even when she's grown. . . .

Contents

1. Why I Write About the Last Three Years of Elvis's Life   1

2. Elvis Explains in His Own Words   8

3. How Priscilla and Elvis and Love Parted   14

4. Lisa Marie and Priscilla Presley Trapped for Life   26

5. Elvis and His Women   32

6. Playgirls, Prostitutes, and Femme Fans   41

7. A Famous Star Reveals Her Night of Love with Elvis   52

8. How Elvis and I Met   55

9. Elvis Reveals All of His Illnesses, Including Cancer   58

10. Elvis Explains His Frequent Solitude and Confides His Frustrations and Desires   69

11. Why Elvis Gave His Famed Diamond Medallion Cross to a Little Fan   79

12. Elvis: A Hero in Action When the Devil Interfered   83

13. Elvis's Temper Tantrums   89

14. Elvis's Questions-and-Answers Legacy   91

15. I Named Elvis "The King" After Clark Gable's Death   106

16. Elvis at MGM and on "The Ed Sullivan Show"   112

17. One Man's View of His Friend Elvis   120

18. Behind the Iron Curtain: Brutal Beatings for Listening to Elvis   126

19. Elvis Tells About the Death of His Mother and Talks About Graceland: "Why It Will Always Be Home"   132

20. "My Visit with Elvis at Graceland" by Bob Wayne   148

21. Aboard Elvis's Luxury Jet, the *Lisa Marie*   156

22. How Elvis Suffered and Died   164

23. The Buzzards Picking Elvis's Dead Flesh   176

24. Friends Lament Elvis's Memory Turned into a Huckster's Carnival   187

25. Love Letters for Elvis to Me   193

26. Epilogue   209

1. Why I Write About the Last Three Years of Elvis's Life

Around three-thirty in the afternoon of a pleasant summer day, August 16, 1977, in California, my telephone rang. The Associated Press news service was calling, asking for any comments I might have: "Elvis Presley just died in Memphis and you were a close friend of his!"

Before I could get over the terrible heart-pounding horror, the shock, my three telephones began ringing incessantly. My stomach twisted into knots and I wanted to throw up. I felt dizzy, my hands turned to ice—I was stunned. I had talked to Elvis just a few days before. . . . Why—how could this have happened?

City desks of newspapers in Los Angeles, New York City, San Francisco, New Jersey, and Dallas called one after another, fairly exploding with questions about Elvis Presley! "You wrote the only authorized biography on Elvis. What can you say about him?"

I was in a comalike state—speechless! Questions poured out of my telephone endlessly. The papers couldn't get to Vernon Presley. Elvis had never had a press agent or a public relations man in his life. He had never had anyone to speak for him. Colonel Parker, who'd never answered questions all through his twenty-two years with Elvis, couldn't be reached. It was well known that Elvis and I had been close friends for twenty years. Photos and snapshots showing us together, as good friends, which had been taken in Hollywood, Las Vegas, and Hawaii over the past eighteen years, had been published from time to time by the news media, hungry for any bits of news on Elvis. So it was that now, I became the one everyone was calling for information.

I'd known for three years that Elvis had been very ill—but dead?

On the heels of the calls from newspaper and TV reporters came a call, then three more, from Japan; then from *Playboy* magazine, then from London, Sweden, Canada, Australia, Germany, Israel, France, and, to my amazement, Soviet Russia. The next day, from Washington, D.C., the White House itself called with a representative of President Carter on the wire.

The best I could do, in my own shock and sadness at losing Elvis, was to refer everyone to our book, Elvis's and mine, which had everything in it, at least everything up to the last three years. And yes, there was so much to report of those last three years of Elvis's life, if only I was in a position to do so. But I was far from this. I was grief-stricken and couldn't talk at all.

No less than four publishers soon called, asking me for another book, to bring the world up to date on Elvis. I declined. I was heartsick to think of it. "Elvis helped me write our book," I told them. "It took us over eighteen years together to write it. Now that he's gone and not here to share it with me, I won't be writing another," I replied.

Fate intervened, however.

A gossip columnist, on that very day of Elvis's death, went on TV and said Elvis had died of an overdose of drugs. This was repeated over and over, pointing toward suicide. How could anyone say that?

Certainly I have no press agent or PR firm, but to my surprise, forty-eight radio shows in the U.S. called me to guest on their one-hour shows, to talk about Elvis and to answer phoned-in questions. I also made six television-show appearances to set the record straight on Elvis, and did numerous newspaper and magazine interviews, all in the name of telling the truth about a man who was not here to defend himself against the continuing malicious lies. At sixteen speaking engagements before large audiences—all gratis: I would not take money—I talked about the Elvis I had known. During these talks I met so many people who wanted to share any knowledge they had of Elvis. They were eager and caring people, people with warmth and sincerity. Some had personal experiences with Elvis to confide. And some had stories to tell about an Elvis they had known even before he became an international superstar.

Requests to tell the truth about Elvis continued to be made, on and on, and still continue to reach me, as interest in the greatest entertainment idol the world has ever known never seems to diminish. When the *Los Angeles Herald-Examiner* city desk first called, on the day Elvis died, asking me to comment, I did manage to say, "The whole world will mourn Elvis as no star since Valentino. Valentino is a legend, with annual Valentino memorials and showings of his

movies fifty years after his death. Valentino did not
have Elvis Presley's records and television specials,
besides the fantastic number of hardworking Elvis
Presley fan clubs. An Elvis Presley fan club in London alone has twelve thousand active members.
Graceland will become a national shrine, like the
Lincoln Memorial and the Washington Monument."

The city desk editor was skeptical. Yet it is all coming readily to pass, with as many as seven thousand
people daily waiting outside the Music Gate of
Graceland, to enter during the visiting hours to see
Elvis's grave in the Meditation Memory Garden,
which Elvis himself had planted and landscaped to
the right of his home. Extra security police are hired
during the vacation season to handle the crowds,
many of whom wait outside the gate and walls all
night to ensure their admittance the next day.

For six months I worked at nothing else, doing all
I could for Elvis, of course without material compen-
sation, being a friend. "A friend in need," as the saying goes, "is a friend indeed." I say this because so
many people asked how much I was being paid. I was
not paid, nor could I have ever even considered ac-
cepting pay.

During this period I received over 4500 letters from
Elvis fans and readers of the newspaper columns and
magazine pieces about Elvis I had written over the
years, as well as from readers of "our book." Each
and every one expressed over and over his or her
grateful appreciation for telling the truth about Elvis.
At the same time, I appeared on two radio "Tributes
to Elvis" on General Electric Flagship's "Bill Miller
Show," WYG, Schenectady, New York—which were
beamed to thirty-seven stations and by satellite, I was
told, to Europe—to talk on all aspects of Elvis's un-

known life, his last three years, and to answer the listeners' phoned-in questions.

Tokyo sent a television crew to my home in California to tape a full hour-long show on Elvis for Japan. I gave endless interviews to all news media.

Bobby Morris, Elvis's conductor/arranger of many years, called me again in the ninth month after Elvis's passing, saying, "May, you were Elvis's very close friend. You must write another book on Elvis. He loved you. He certainly said so many times. Everyone's been writing on Elvis who never knew him. You owe it to yourself and to Elvis to do it. As you well know, I spent a great amount of time with Elvis, and he talked about you so much. I'll help all I can."

Month after month since Elvis's death, the mail still keeps pouring in from all over the world. Long, long letters from fans who had seen him in concert and fans who had never seen him but adore him in movies and on records. What and who Elvis was—and is—comes into clear focus in these letters, which arrive from all over the United States, Canada, South America, Scotland, Ireland, France, Sweden, Germany, Japan—everywhere.

A typical example is the letter I received in February 1978 from C.T., of Aurora, Colorado; here is an excerpt: "My heart is so full of things I want to say, I don't know where to begin. I so enjoyed Elvis as a performer and that's the way he remains in my heart. While I was never able to get to know him as a real person, now, through your *Elvis and the Colonel* and *The Private Elvis,* I know more about the wonderful performer who has thrilled me so, and he has now become much more to me. Through your book I realize more than ever that he was really an open, warm, and loving man who cared about people. Other stars never seem interested in us. They remain untouched and distant, but not Elvis. He started out caring and never quit. Through you, at least he has become real, and in a sense I feel I've touched him and know him in a way I never thought possible. You have opened a window and let in fresh air and sunlight. It's nice to know he was never a disappointment in any way. Thousands of his followers are furious at the lies written about him. Thank you, for you were a ray of sunshine for him, someone who really cared for the man he was, instead of 'the image' he represented. You wrote about him up to the last three years of his life. Won't you please write the rest and share him with us again? Thank you."

Here is another letter, K.M.S., North Carolina: "I'm twenty-seven years old, the wife of a deputy sheriff, a mother of two children, and a loyal fan of Elvis Presley. Your book was a refreshing piece of facts, facts that were so long held back from all of us. Your sharing your life with Elvis with us is unique. Won't you please write the rest of it? In so many stories I read about Elvis after his death, I see that for some reason his critics wanted to punish him, and not accept Elvis as a human being. The drug rumor has cut a wound, a deep wound that has really hurt his family. Thousands of us Elvis fans want to do something about it and don't know what to do. But you can. Will you?

"Since Elvis's death my husband has apologized to me for not taking me to see one of his concerts. He's promised to take me to Graceland this year. There wasn't a single age group that could not enjoy his kind of entertainment. May, everyone could. My mother is fifty-seven years old. She watches and reads everything about him. Like me, she too has all of his records, posters, and also some of the tributes paid him by other artists. When Elvis got married, he said it was for good, and I figured any girl in her right mind would make sure it was forever. Most girls loved him because he was a superstar and wealthy perhaps, but I loved him in spite of it. My husband understands now the feeling I have had all these years for Elvis and has tried to comfort me. But in spite of all of that, I feel a large part of me is missing and always will be. You were so close to him. Please write, telling us the rest of the inside, intimate side of Elvis's life until his death. Please tell us the truth of his death."

This was my dilemma. What was I to do?

2. Elvis Explains in His Own Words

As I have said, publishers called asking me to rush a new Elvis Presley book to them. This was just days after Elvis's death. I had already written a book on Elvis, *with* Elvis, when he was alive—and I had no intention of writing another one. I was too upset over his death, over the loss to the world of such a fine person. It was even more upsetting to learn that already so many people were writing books and trying to find faults with him—to sensationalize their experiences for money.

My first thoughts were for Vernon Presley and Priscilla and Lisa Marie—the heartbreak they must be going through over such a loss.

I received a thank-you letter from Vernon Presley in reply to my condolences. Dated September 14, 1977, it read: "Thank you for your letter and card. It was so thoughtful of you. We do appreciate your friendship with Elvis, and the article you did also. I'm sorry about the mix-up in the mails so that you had to remail the letter. Again thank you, and God bless you. Sincerely, Vernon Presley."

From Priscilla, in her beautiful handwriting, dated August 26, 1977, came the following words: "Dear May: You were kind to think of us at such a truly difficult time. Your thoughtful card was comforting and deeply appreciated. Sincerely, Priscilla and Lisa Presley."

That was the start of the avalanche of mail from people—people all over the world who loved Elvis, who knew what he stood for and what he was. So many had read my book. They all are nice, wholesome, wonderful people—I could tell this by the way they expressed themselves in their letters. After receiving five thousand—and they are still continuing—I felt deeply about not being able to reply to all of them. *How could I?* It would take a great deal of money, which I did not have. And it would take months also to reply to them all.

It was when the letters asking me to write another book on Elvis, began to arrive, the letters pleading with me to tell the truth about all of the false accusations and set the record straight about what really happened to him, that nine months after his passing, I decided to write this book. It has taken me five years to complete. It is written for all those who wrote such wonderful letters. There was not one dissenter in all of them.

The appreciation of people for Elvis, people who were willing to stand and wait at my speaking engagements sometimes for many hours for the chance to tell me their own experiences with Elvis, is indeed treasured by me, and I share what they told me here with you. More than anything else, these many untold stories of Elvis Presley helped me decide to finally write this book.

As I write, I have received to date 5,452 letters from Elvis fans since Elvis's passing. It is letters like this one—and letters from people of all ages—that encourage me to continue setting the record straight on Elvis Presley.

This 1978 letter from a young Hollywood, Florida, fan, which is so typical of so many, reads: "I just want you to know how much I enjoyed your book, *The Private Elvis*. I think it was one of the most truthful books I've ever read. I'm fifteen years old. I was too young to know who Elvis was when he was at the height of his career—even though his career was never low. I can remember watching the Elvis from Hawaii special on TV and seeing lots of his movies on the summer late shows during 1974 and '75. Watching Elvis's movies got me hooked on Elvis, and when I learned of his death, I was so terribly shocked. I never thought of Elvis dying. He was so young, and the future, I'm sure, held many wonderful things ahead.

"I am hoping that you could write a new book about Elvis telling of his death; the real cause of it, what caused him to get so out of shape, the truth behind the Ginger Alden marriage rumors, etc. I'm very curious and I'm sure other Elvis fans are. Once again, I truly enjoyed your book. LONG LIVE THE KING!!"

Yes, young man, it's all here, I hope all that you want to know, and more.

Almost daily, new information from close, reliable sources kept coming to me. People who knew Elvis. So many, many wonderful intimate experiences with Elvis for me to share.

Elvis himself, realizing he was so ill, had told me he had put messages on his tape recorder for his little Lisa Marie, "so when she grows up she'll know that her daddy thought of her, loved her, and wanted so much for her. And I believe," Elvis said during one of our last talks, "that she will know her daddy as he was—not from hearsay. If that time comes, I know you will set the record straight for me."

"Elvis," I said, "that will be likely ten years from now—or more."

"Oh no"—he sighed—"much sooner, much, much sooner than you think." He didn't say he was dying, but I knew he knew. . . .

Elvis was very intuitive, and I feel sure he knew it was happening to him, and soon. After all, he had been in the hospital so many times in these last three years, trying to overcome, to beat fate—and he was losing. He read medical books. He employed a doctor on a twenty-four-hours-a-day basis, full-time. But Elvis was getting worse instead of better. Always when Elvis talked to me he was upbeat—always on the bright side. Sometimes he did admit that being a Capricorn, he had low depressions like all of us—and a great deal of loneliness too.

I think Elvis's true feelings are so beautifully expressed in the prose he often wrote but felt no one would want to read. He wrote a beautiful farewell to his father for Christmas in 1975, less than two years before his passing. This was a very special message, for Elvis had given his father everything money could buy—and his "daddy," as Elvis always called him in speaking of his father to me—had given Elvis his complete devotion and love.

Elvis's lovely spirit shines through in the handwritten epistle to Vernon Presley, which is framed and holds a place of honor in Vernon's home. I can only quote from memory, so the words might not be exactly right. It reads something like this: "To Dad: I not only live for today, but for the day after today. I have pursued my vision and reached the mountain-top. But the peak of a mountain can be a lonely place. I want to thank you for understanding." Elvis wrote that early in his life he had learned that it was only by directing existence toward a goal that he could find any inner peace and fulfillment. He told his father he wanted to thank him for giving him intangible gifts. "You gave me gifts from your heart—understanding, tolerance, and concern. You gave me gifts of your words—encouragement, empathy and solace."

"Respect," Elvis wrote, "wants to contain everything." And for his father, his friend, his confidant, he had an avid respect.

"Thanks for always being near the top of the mountain, when I needed you. Your son, Elvis."

Such inner thoughts expressed and written by Elvis truly unveils the soul, and the beauty of the soul, of the man.

To all who knew Elvis Presley slightly or met him in person, those who saw him in concert or the thirty-two motion pictures he starred in, or the eight television specials he filmed, or simply knew *of* him—the escalating millions of men, women, and children of all ages from six to eighty who have bought and are still buying his records, and to the thousands of people who have personally written to me and the thousands more who met me or called me—to those who knew him well and those who loved him but never met him—all those asking for the rest of the inside intimate Elvis—to complete the cycle of his life ... *Here it is.*

By all of your requests, this book of the last three years of Elvis's personal untold life, his death, and also after his death—the truth, complete with Elvis's own words—is written for you.

Due to the many *totally false* allegations and misconceptions, the appearance of which Elvis himself had prophetically foreseen and warned me about, it is necessary to set the record straight.

3. How Priscilla and Elvis and Love Parted

"Elvis, are you getting married now, I hear?"

"No." He laughed over the telephone. "May, you've been asking me, am I in love and am I getting married to at least a half-dozen women over the years. The only one you never asked me that question about was Cilla. And I was as surprised as you were when it happened."

The girl now in question was beauty-contest winner Ginger Alden, who had a $50,000 diamond ring from Elvis.

Elvis was noncommittal. "No, I'm not getting married. I would like to—if I could find a girl with no ambitions to become an actress. I can't find even one who wants to be with me, be my full-time wife and companion."

"Elvis, come on now. You can have your pick of thousands."

"Maybe, but not one for me. It's like having a lakeful of water, and not one glass to drink.

"I want children, at least two or three more. Years ago I told you I wanted several children. I'm running out of time. Lisa Marie will soon be ten. Like me, she's always longing for a brother or sister. As a kid I used to go over to my twin brother Jesse Garon's grave and think about him, and wish he was here."

With his usual swift change of tone and mood, Elvis said, "I have to be a playmate and a little kid with Lisa Marie. I enjoy it. She doesn't have anyone to play with here. I get down on the floor and play all sorts of kid games with her. She's smarter than I am at most of them."

"No wedding bells with Ginger?"

Elvis didn't reply.

A couple of years before, when I asked Elvis if he was marrying Linda Thompson, also a beauty-contest winner, he'd said, "We are buddies—that's better. She's very intelligent, very religious. We have a lot in common. She's good company. She understands me. But Linda wants to be an actress. You see how it is. I want a girl who just wants to be my wife. If I can ever find a girl like that, I'll grab her and marry her. You'll be sure of that.

"I love kids, I love babies, watching them grow up. My little girl is growing up so fast. She keeps saying, when I ask her what she wants most in all the world, 'A baby brother.'

" 'I'll accept a baby sister,' she said the other day. She plays dolls. Lisa will make a good little mama, she really will."

Turning serious, Elvis said. "I pray about it a lot. I get very lonely. I've always wanted very much to have a marriage like my mama and my daddy. They had each other and they didn't need anyone else to make them happy. They had real love. Well, someday

. . ." Elvis left the words hanging. One thing I ascertained: there was not one girl in his life, the few weeks before his death, whom he planned to marry. Not one.

When Elvis was twenty-two, he and I had a long talk about love. Elvis didn't laugh it off, as he would do later on.

I still remember the hurt coming to play in his eyes when he told me, "I was in love with a girl who lived in the settlement apartments where we did. I was very serious. I thought I'd marry her someday. I'd rush home from school and knock on her door, as I'd see her every day. When I got to driving a truck and being away so much, and when I started singing a little here and there, she took up with another fellow. It hurt. It hurt bad for a long, long time.

"Even now, my heart hurts when I think of it. When I sing, 'Love me tender, love me true, all my dreams fulfill,' I am singing from my heart. You don't fool around with your heart. I haven't been that in love since. I got so badly hurt that once, and that was when I was just plain me. . . . I didn't have anything but my beat-up old car to drive around, that was always stopping on me. Now when I have Cadillacs—how will I ever know that a girl will love me for myself? The truth is I am afraid to trust my heart and get hurt again.

"It's sad—a sad way to be—isn't it?" he remarked thoughtfully. "If I ever find a girl who is all 100 percent for me—who wants to be with me all of my life and not run off, who will always be home waiting for me when I come home, then I'll let my little old heart go all the way."

I thought Anita Wood, a pretty Memphis girl who kissed him openly, dated him in Memphis, and visited

him in Hollywood, was his real love. She was not.
There were two actresses in Germany who were
madly in love with Elvis. He dated them until he saw
them exploiting their dates as publicity in the press,
with photographers always taking pictures wherever
they went.

I asked, "Who is Priscilla?" When Elvis first returned from the army. He laughed. "She's not a romance, why she's only fifteen. She's like a cute little
kid sister."

Each year I'd ask Elvis again, although it seemed
superfluous to ask about Priscilla since he was dating
Connie Stevens, Ann-Margret, and Juliet Prowse
when he was in Hollywood. And in Memphis, he saw
his hometown girl friends.

I'd see photos of Elvis with Vernon and his wife
Dee and there would be this beautiful teenager, Priscilla, with them.

"Cilla's like one of the family," he'd remind me.

Suddenly, out of the blue, they were married! Elvis
said later that he'd entertained the idea at times.
"Priscilla is intelligent, has class, she's petite and
pretty—very pretty—but I hadn't thought actually of
getting married for a long, long time. Then Colonel
Parker was saying, 'You can't have Priscilla living at
Graceland now. She's twenty-one. It's better you get
married.'

" 'My grandmother lives here, and my aunt,' I re-
minded him. 'Priscilla's plenty chaperoned!'

" 'Her father thinks you should marry her. It's
time!' he replied.

"The next thing I knew Colonel Parker had arranged the wedding and all the details in Las Vegas. I
didn't have time to second-thought getting married at
all. This was it. Priscilla's a lovely girl," he said. "I

am sure she knows me well enough over these last few years—so our marriage will be forever. Besides, we have Lisa Marie, and I hope we have at least six kids."

After Elvis's death, suddenly, the news media were seeking interviews with Priscilla. Where was she, how did she meet Elvis? Were they ever truly in love? What broke them up? Priscilla was now the focal point of interest in Elvis Presley's family. She was his only wife, even if she was an ex-wife. Furthermore, she was the mother of Elvis's only child.

Being polite, Priscilla responded to their questions, though as briefly as possible. She was the daughter of Captain Joseph P. Beaulieu of the United States Air Force. She had brothers and a sister. She was born in Brooklyn, New York, on May 24, 1945. Yes, she had been an Elvis fan. Her father was transferred to Wiesbaden, Germany, where they learned Elvis was in the army's Third Armored Division near Bad Nauheim. Priscilla hoped for a chance to catch a glimpse of him—maybe even meet him. Her mother was in agreement. Priscilla was fourteen at the time. Elvis was nine years older.

Lamar Fike and Red West, two of Elvis's boys who were with him in Germany, kept an eye peeled for a new girl for Elvis to meet. Priscilla, though petite, looked older than her fourteen years. At a favorite GI restaurant, one of the boys glimpsed Priscilla and decided she'd be nice to know. He invited her to come to Elvis's house for an informal party. Priscilla was as excited after meeting Elvis that night as any teenager would be. Her father disapproved of her going again. Her mother disagreed. Permission was given provided she was home before a set curfew of twelve midnight. One of Elvis's boys would call for, pick her up, escort her to the Presley house, and take her home. When Elvis received his discharge, Priscilla was distraught. To Elvis, she was like a little kid sister. Priscilla, however, had other dreams. When they said good-bye, Elvis told her when her family returned to the States to come to Graceland and say hello.

On Elvis's departure, Priscilla found herself a local celebrity overnight. She was being asked, actually widely sought, for interviews and pictures because she was an American girl in Germany who'd known Elvis Presley. Pictures of her holding a picture of Elvis were run in the German newspapers and were published in the United States.

Elvis saw the photos, heard from Priscilla, and called her. During their conversation he suddenly asked if she'd like to come to Graceland for Christmas. An immediate yes was the reply. After her visit, Priscilla, suddenly accustomed to the luxury and excitement of living at Graceland with the Vernon Presleys and Grandma Presley, wanted to return. Finally, she obtained the consent of her parents to attend school in Memphis. For the next four years, she did just that. She was Elvis's kid sister, and he bought her two or three little bright-colored cars of her own to drive on her successive birthdays, until he felt she was grown up enough to have a white Mercedes.

Elvis never realized that his dates with Natalie Wood, Tuesday Weld, Ann-Margret, and Juliet Prowse in Hollywood during his stays making movies, caused "Cilla", as he called "the little kid sister" at home, much heartache and jealousy.

And then, one day, Priscilla was twenty-one. Colonel Parker announced it would be a good idea if they got married. It was not right for a grown-up young lady like Priscilla to live at Graceland without a wedding ring. Overnight, Elvis once told me, he found himself a bridegroom at a big wedding at the Aladdin Hotel in Las Vegas—all commandered by the Colonel.

"I had always thought of a church wedding and my bride walking down the aisle in white. Mama used to look at wedding books, and she'd keep planning the kind of wedding she wanted for my bride. Mama never had a little girl of her own. I believed Mama would have loved Priscilla when I married her. And I wanted children. I love children—lots of them."

Priscilla left Elvis in February 1972. The reason, she later told me one afternoon in her new shop, "Bis and Beau," in Beverly Hills, was "Because I couldn't stand living in prison—with bodyguards all of the time. Elvis and I rarely ever had any time alone—it was always his boys [the "Memphis Mafia"] around—in our home [in Beverly Hills]. It was never *our* home—but always other people living with us. It can become suffocating, never to have any freedom. And every time you stick your nose out, there are photographers waiting to snap pictures. Always there are people standing around staring into your windows through binoculars—hundreds of fans—some of them stayed in campers and vans—living day and night in front of our honeymoon house in Beverly Hills. You couldn't open a window even without having all the clamor outside. You did not have any privacy whatsoever. . . . It was like being in a cage, like monkeys in a zoo. And constantly being stared at. Graceland was almost the same, except a little further removed from the road.

"Elvis was more than generous [in the divorce settlement]. I could have all the money to spend I wanted, have any and everything I wanted. What can

you do with closets full of clothes and no place to go
to wear them?

"Elvis gave me beautiful jewelry—but you don't
wear jewelry around the house. I was always redecorating one of our four homes, or going shopping—but
that can become humdrum, doing it alone. Elvis was
gone much of the time on tour. When he came home,
he was enveloped with his recording and business
people.

"I just had to express my own self, my own personality, be my own person. I wasn't happy with his life,
although I loved Elvis. And I always will."

Priscilla had invited me, by a handwritten note, to
the opening party of her boutique. I had accepted
but then I came down with the flu and called back
and politely said I had to decline.

Later we met. And one day she came to my house
for lunch and we talked again. Priscilla is a girl with
class as well as beauty. She is very intelligent. As Elvis
said, she also has a strong mind of her own.

Once, a few years earlier, when she was still married to Elvis, I had asked Priscilla if she would put on
a charity fund-raising fashion show and she had
graciously accepted. The event was held at the Century Plaza Hotel, and it was packed. People adored
seeing Groucho Marx and his girl friend, Erin Flem-
ing, and a host of major stars on the dais. But mostly,
they were fascinated seeing Priscilla Presley in person.
As mistress of ceremonies, in charge of introducing
the celebrities, I sat between Max Baer, Jr., and Priscilla. Maxie attempted to chat with Priscilla, who
seemed highly nervous and had little to say. She had
lived Elvis's life for so long—hiding away from the
general public until it had become a part of her.
When the news photographers clustered around her
to take pictures, she did not smile. I think she pre-

tended they were not there. And suddenly, when I began introducing the stars, before I could introduce Priscilla, she had fled. Backstage I found her, her usual, polite, lovely self.

Priscilla returned and did narrate her fashion show after all, her English articulate and better-sounding than that of the most professionally trained actresses. Her gown—indeed, the whole show—was the most glamorous that Los Angeles, Beverly Hills, and Bel Air had ever seen. Priscilla wore a white silk blouse underneath a navy-blue sheath, and what with her natural beauty, was a real delight. Elvis later said he was very proud of her and the fashion show. However, Priscilla never repeated her personal appearance or a show—no matter the flood of requests. "It was too public," she said. She had been a recluse with Elvis too long.

From what Elvis remarked to me, I never thought he was really deeply in love with Priscilla—not the kind of love a man has to have to marry a woman. He loved her, yes—but more like a little sister than a wife. She had been just that to him for years: a kid sister. When it was suggested they should get married—well, Elvis did want children. He had known Priscilla all those years she had lived in Memphis and had become a part of the family. Since there was no other girl whom Elvis had fallen deeply in love with, Priscilla was a very likely candidate. Elvis himself said that the wedding was arranged almost as a surprise to him. He wasn't sure he wanted to be married at that particular point in his life, but at the same time, he always planned to marry someday for he especially did want children.

When the break came, Priscilla told him that there was now another man in her life. It surprised Elvis that she had fallen in love with the karate instructor he paid to teach her the fine points of the art. Elvis, who believed firmly that Priscilla and he would be married "until death do us part," was deeply shocked, then deeply hurt. His pride was badly hurt as well.

Priscilla was not a gold digger. She had a great respect and affection for Elvis. She told him she did not want to "take" him, and it was up to him to make a fair settlement, just enough so she could live comfortably. Elvis asked whether, if he gave her $1000 a month for herself and $500 for Lisa Marie—who would spend as much time as possible with him at Graceland, according to his attorney—that would be fair. It seemed especially fair since there was already a new man in her life, whom she might marry.

Priscilla did not start dating the most eligible men in the world—which was naturally expected of her. After all, she had already been married to the idol of millions. First there was Mike Stone, the Hawaiian karate instructor who had a wife and children and obtained a divorce so he could be free to be with Priscilla.

Next came her hairdresser, Elie Ezerzer, a handsome, dark-eyed twenty-nine-year-old of French Moroccan parentage, who had been raised in Paris. He was the man Priscilla said she loved a few months before Elvis died. Elie said, "I'm not a live-in boyfriend. Someday we hope to marry. But we are together all of the time." They had met when she was under a Beverly Hills beauty-shop hairdryer.

Priscilla was always very smart. After the divorce, she never, at any time, tried to influence Lisa Marie to dislike any of Elvis's girl friends. That way, they all loved Lisa Marie and really cared for her—for the child spent a lot of time with her daddy. Priscilla is a wise mother. She placed the welfare of her child first and foremost rather than showing any feelings she might have about any girl who was replacing her with Elvis.

Elvis was so upset when his wife flew up to Las Vegas and told him she was having a romance with Mike Stone. She didn't have to tell him, but she did. She was honest and had the integrity not to try to fool him. That night Elvis could hardly do his show. In fact, he cut his show short, so short some people asked for their money back. Elvis explained, "My little old heart has just had the shock and hurt of my life!" I don't think he ever got over losing Priscilla. Southern men marry but once in general, and their little women stay home and wait for their return. Priscilla hadn't followed the pattern, and Elvis had fully expected she would.

Their marriage had lasted seven years. Elvis was now thirty-seven and Priscilla twenty-eight. Lisa Marie was four years of age. In 1973 Elvis finally sued for divorce.

What Elvis dreaded the most, however, was yet to come. The property settlement he and Priscilla signed was not adequate, according to her new lawyer. She filed a new suit to obtain a fair division of community property, stating she had lived with Elvis and his family since she was sixteen and never knew anything about his finances, even when she signed income-tax papers. She, who had had all of the money she ever wanted, soon realized, she said, that she could not live on $1500 a month in the style she and Lisa Marie had grown accustomed to during her marriage to Elvis.

Elvis, in reply, said he had agreed to Priscilla's list of monthly expenses and that Priscilla had telephoned him twice from Hawaii, where she was staying with Mike Stone, saying she had quarreled with Mike and wanted to come home to Elvis. Elvis told her he was not a fixture, nor could she take him for granted. And since there had been no fraud intended on either side—Priscilla was fortunately awarded a generous settlement which made her an instant millionairess. While her friendship with Mr. Stone continued, it did not, as I have said, end up in marriage.

Elvis remained friendly, however, with Priscilla until his death. After Elvis's death Priscilla felt it necessary for her lawyer to file a new suit for her claim for three quarters of a million dollars still due her. Priscilla asked for $744,907.93, stating that Elvis still owed her $365,908 from her 1973 divorce settlement. She also requested 5 percent of the total stock of the Elvis Presley Music Company, plus $4000 a month for their daughter, Lisa Marie, plus other expenses, plus attorney fees.

Vernon Presley, conservator of Elvis's estate, replied to this by claiming that Elvis had provided all of these monies through life-insurance policies and through provisions in his will for his heir, Lisa Marie.

But money alone can never conpensate Priscilla and Lisa Marie for what they must endure for the rest of their lives: they are trapped, virtual prisoners of Elvis Presley's fame and fortune.

4. Lisa Marie and Priscilla Presley Trapped for Life

The pendulum of fate swings. Priscilla left Elvis because she could no longer stand her lack of freedom and her secluded, prisonlike life, could no longer endure being guarded and watched twenty-four hours a day by security men. This was the price of fate imposed on Elvis during those twenty-two years of his fame. Now the same fate has grasped and closed in on Priscilla and her and Elvis's child, Lisa Marie. As long as Priscilla and Lisa Marie Presley live, they will never know either the relaxation or the peace of free people.

Little Lisa Marie is a rich young heiress. Will Priscilla and Lisa Marie ever have peace of mind, in view of the many kidnap threats that beset the child? With Elvis alive to protect them, they had a large measure of security. Without Elvis, they are a beautiful woman and a little girl—alone against the world.

On that fateful August day when Elvis Presley died, Lisa Marie, who had been having the time of her life at Graceland with her father as her playmate—and expected to continue having him all of her school summer vacation—heard a terrible commotion. Pounding footsteps were running up and down the hallway and the stairways. She ran into Elvis's bedroom to learn what was happening. Seeing Elvis lying prostrate on the floor, with a doctor giving mouth-to-mouth resuscitation, is a scene which will flash with horror in her mind forever. As will the sight of her grandfather Vernon sobbing, "Everything's gone. My son, my son, my son." Lisa Marie rushed over to touch her father, screaming, "Daddy, Daddy, wake up!"

The tragic trauma she suffered in those seconds stamped her entire life. She can never forget. Someone grabbed her and rushed her out of the room. Breaking loose, she ran shrieking hysterically down the hall, then down the stairs, all the while screaming, "My daddy's dead! My daddy's dead!"

Grandma Presley, then in her eighties, was beside herself with grief, and tried to hold on to the child to soothe her. It was to no avail. Little Lisa Marie, who looks like Elvis in miniature—the same blue eyes, the same smile—ran screaming from room to room. She did not know who to go to—whose arms to run to for support, who she could reach out to for comfort. Always, there had been her daddy, Elvis.

Vernon immediately sent to California for Priscilla, who was en route to her home from a California health spa, La Costa. During the weekend there, Priscilla, always meticulous about maintaining her slender figure, had lost four pounds. Reaching her Beverly Hills home, she learned the news. Vernon would send the *Lisa Marie,* Elvis's private jet, for her at once. No, it was quicker for Priscilla to board the

next Los Angeles airliner for Memphis. Her hairdresser, who was to become the new man in her life,
drove her to the airport.

Priscilla found herself deluged by questions from
the news media the minute she stepped onto
Tennessee soil. After a couple of hours of attempting
to stop the tears of hysteria and heartbreak of her
little daughter, she took over the chaos of Graceland.
Systematically, Priscilla began organizing relatives
and friends, making plans, assisting Vernon with funeral arrangements, and presiding as lady of the
manor to the many people arriving from and depart-
ing in all directions.

Through all of this, however, consoling Lisa Marie
was her constant task. Priscilla, now thirty-one years
of age, had matured into a lovely woman. She had
the wisdom and the desire to become the close companion of her daughter, to make an attempt to re-
place the remarkable companion Elvis had always
been to his child with herself. Vernon wanted Lisa
Marie left at Graceland. But Priscilla took her home
to Beverly Hills.

Thousands of people descended on Graceland to
mourn Elvis, whose God-given gifts, talent, sweetness
of character, actual humility—his sharing of all he
had, his strength to go on and not disappoint his
loved ones and his fans—had so impressed and
marked their own lives. And with it all came the
scavangers and all their hoopla, selling all kinds of
junky Elvis souvenirs to make a fast buck. And with
it also came an even greater need for tighter security
for Lisa Marie. No matter where she might be—it was
now known that she had inherited over $150 million.
Evil people, hungry to get some of that Elvis gold,

one way or another, hatched nefarious plots. The quickest way would be to kidnap Lisa Marie.

Priscilla, near to distraction with fear for her daughter's safety, secretly took Lisa Marie to Europe, in the hopes of placing her in a good school where she could have a free life and a greater sense of security—away from the United States and the threats. Priscilla also hoped that by sight-seeing and touring she would be able to district Lisa Marie from her grief and ease the pain and the tragic memory in the little girl's now unlaughing, somber eyes.

Lisa Marie, despite that daily panorama of new places to explore in Europe, had all but forgotten how to smile. In spite of all the distractions, the child remained somber. And always, of course, there had to be bodyguards and tight security with Priscilla and her Lisa Marie twenty-four hours of the day. Guards with guns had to sleep outside their bedroom at night. Lisa Marie would awaken from nightmares, sobbing. Not only the nights in her sleep, but waking days were one long, terrible nightmare to endure. When would it ever end? Or could it?

Even more painful were the rejections by schools in Italy, England, and Switzerland, among others, who reportedly refused to consider Lisa Marie as a live-in student. The security risk would be too great. Italy had been plagued with dozens of kidnappings, which had led to multimillion-dollar ransoms being paid, only to find the dead body of the kidnapped. It was a gruesome situation. The whole world had gone crazy. Priscilla and Lisa Marie returned home. Where in the world was there a safe place for them to be?

What they called home was now a fortress. Police dogs, trained to kill intruders, guarded the frightened mother and child; the house and gates were wired, while the faces of anyone approaching the house, even at a considerable distance were flashed by cameras onto screens inside. The slightest sound set the dogs to barking and sent fear into the heart of Priscilla.

No longer could Lisa Marie have playmates or go to other children's homes for slumber parties or stay-overs. She was now a valuable object—a little girl hunted, because her father had died and left her one of the richest little girls in the world. And all of those hungry, wild, killer wolves in human forms were stalking outside the domain of her hired security men, waiting to get her.

No longer could Priscilla go about freely—to shop, to drive out her front gates with Lisa Marie for one reason or another—without the fear of being followed. Maybe not now, today, maybe not tomorrow, but sometime—*when*? The tensions built and built. Elvis's death had placed Priscilla in a prison more confining than any even Elvis ever knew.

Priscilla never allowed anyone to come inside the gates of their home, even the closest members of her family unless they were first scanned carefully on the inside camera screens of her house. Even then, after receiving clearance by this means, security went out to admit them to make sure no one with a gun was hiding behind them, ready to break in.

No longer could Priscilla walk outside and freely invite people to visit or simply greet them in a normal, friendly way. Her world had almost become a world of total aloneness, her isolation far far greater than it had been when Elvis lived.

Fate had indeed taken a strange, strange hand in reversing the roles of Elvis and Priscilla. A strange, cruel, and ironic hand.

For Priscilla's decision to leave Elvis in the first place had been motivated by that very kind of confinement, the confinement imposed by sharing Elvis's life in that so-called ivory tower of his success: always having bodyguards, always running in and out of public places, never being at ease and free to go about, never able to share and participate in life; always being cooped up in a house or a hotel room—a prisoner of the fabulous Elvis Presley fame. Now it had happened to Priscilla, and through no doing of her own. And it had happened as well to the little, innocent girl who had been—and is—the true, real happiness of the storybook marriage of the King Elvis and the beautiful, Cinderella Princess Priscilla.

5. Elvis and His Women

"Women of all ages, all sizes, all complexions, all races were after Elvis," Jim Seagrave, publicity director of Caesar's Palace in Las Vegas, tells me. We were reminiscing about when we had first met. I had come up to Las Vegas to see Elvis, who loved Silver City and often drove there for weekends during his long movie-making days in Hollywood. Now Elvis had died and Jim and I sat over a long lunch remembering Elvis.

"I was PR man at the Aladdin Hotel in the late sixties," Jim recalled, "before the International Hotel opened. Colonel Parker, who was a great friend of Milton Prell, the owner of the Aladdin, was up here a lot of times negotiating with Bill Miller and Alex Shoofey for Elvis's Las Vegas opening. This was his first appearance since his initial Vegas debut at the New Frontier many years before. Elvis was very public in those days. He had been so confined while making his first set of three motion pictures a year in

Hollywood. So Elvis was on holiday, enjoying himself, being free and getting about with people.

"We had a show with The Lady Birds, a topless, all-girl band. It was not a superstar attraction, but Elvis saw the show and invited the whole troupe to be his guests for dinner at a gourmet restaurant. We didn't have overwhelming star shows in the casino at the Aladdin then, for it only had 350 rooms. And Elvis was free and easy with everyone who stopped him in the casino, where he loved to play blackjack. Elvis was extremely friendly and open. He would stand in the lobby sometimes and sign autographs for an hour at a time."

It was impossible not to notice during these times that women were coming in from all over, all seeking to meet Elvis. Even some of the stars appearing in Vegas, the biggest names included would offer a $100 tip to find out when Elvis was in town and where they could run into him. Photographers and agents also offered generous tips; one agent offered $1000 if he could get a picture of his star client with Elvis!

"Taking photos with Elvis was forbidden by Colonel Parker, and Elvis would have to bow out of any such propositions," Jim Seagrave continued. "He'd be so gentlemanly and gracious about it, even the biggest superfemme stars didn't get their feelings upset by the necessary turndown. Of course when he opened later at the International, there was supervised, rigid control enforced. People just couldn't get to Elvis at all. Mostly he stayed in his penthouse suite all of the time, only coming down for show time.

"We noted at the Aladdin however," Jim recalled, "that Elvis usually ate his meals in his room. And somewhere between the kitchen and the bellhops and his room, after any meal, the trays would return empty. No cups, saucers, plates or silver. They had been siphoned off by some ambitious waiter or whoever, to sell to fans, or by hotel employees who idolized Elvis and wanted to keep any possible memento—one that Elvis had actually used. The same with pillow slips, towels, and sheets—they seemed to walk off by themselves. The hotel was aware that souvenir seekers were the cause. Since so many hundreds of people were attracted to the hotel in the hope of glimpsing Elvis, no one protested.

"Elvis was a real nice guy, friendly and warm and well liked by everyone," Jim said. He never saw Elvis much or talked to him after this time, for Jim left to become publicity director of the Flamingo.

In my talks with other hotel employees who had access to Elvis and his Memphis Mafia during his engagements, the fact that those close to Elvis would take large tips was freely discussed. These tips kept getting bigger, much bigger, on the promise that an introduction to Elvis Presley would be made. Some of the people who often shopped for him were reported to have hiked up the prices of even the most incidental purchases they made for Elvis, who would never know the difference, since he couldn't go into the stores to buy things himself. There was never anything like blackmail involved—just downright thievery, one said. "I couldn't snitch on the rest," one told me, "because I worked with them. But they thought they had everything coming to them—and why not!"

When I was appearing at the book fair at the Ambassador Hotel, courtesy of Margaret Burk, many people came to me to report or to tell me their own personal incidents and experiences, if they had been so lucky as to meet Elvis in the flesh. One was a gentleman blackjack dealer from Las Vegas. "Elvis used to come in sometimes in the early-morning hours and play at my table. He was a very intelligent boy, and he often won. Whenever he won Elvis always put a $100 bill in my shirt pocket. No one else ever did that. It seemed like he wanted to always share everything. I got a lot of $100 bills that way, all from Elvis."

The maitres d' at the hotels where Elvis appeared, according to more than one waiter, received all sorts of big tips, often as much as $100, for a ringside seat, "to get close to Elvis." Especially the fan clubs, whose members would charter special planes and fly in from places like Japan, Germany, Holland, England, France, and Canada—fans who saved their earnings for a year to make this trip—would attend Elvis's show every night for a week. They'd pay extravagant tips to ensure their place near the front of the stage.

The luscious stars appearing at other hotels in Las Vegas sent Elvis the most pressing invitations: "Please join me after the midnight show!" One wrote a love note that never even reached Elvis. She is a dazzling beauty, spoiled and accustomed to having her own way with men. She couldn't get through to Elvis on the telephone, which was always monitored by the Memphis Mafia. So she sent a note in a basket of red roses, which read: "Darling, I will be waiting for you tonight in my suite, wearing something so sheer, and with my perfumed body waiting so anxiously for yours. I hope you will cut your show as short as possible, and come to me." She boldly signed her name. Elvis never saw her letter. Many such love missives from superstars, secretaries, maids, working girls, and fans were intercepted and never delivered to Elvis. The legal and security forces that formed Elvis's entourage protected him from any such rendezvous, in fear of traps, bad publicity, dreamed-up paternity suits, and the like. Elvis was kept from alleged harm even when, on some occasions, he might have wished to be protected less.

On occasional nights during his regular, twice-a-year engagement at the International Hilton, Elvis would sometimes say to his orchestra leader, Bobby Morris: "If you see a real nice girl—someone refined, intelligent, and very nice, then I'd like you to bring her over and introduce her to me."

"Elvis always stressed a *nice* girl. He was aware of the scheming, conniving ones who wanted to use him for thrills," said Bobby, "or for publicity, to splash his name with theirs in all of the columns as a big, hot love affair." Seldom were any such rumors ever reported in the news about Elvis. He was careful about his associations—as he said, liking only nice, young ladies he could trust.

"Elvis was seldom alone or on his own when he visited the late spots in Las Vegas on rare occasions. Usually a couple of his guards were with him. And sometimes, a few show people including local show girls. He was generous and sensitive to the point of never wanting to hurt anyone's feelings, especially when someone in the business asked, 'Oh, Elvis, please can we join you?' Elvis always took the check too, for their midnight suppers and snacks—even when he couldn't join them."

After his marriage to Priscilla ended, Elvis began seeing Linda Thompson, a tall, curvaceous, five-foot-nine-inch beauty-contest winner from Memphis. Linda was clever. She never tried to tie Elvis down or allowed herself to show any jealousy. When he met other beauties who asked to join Linda and him, she was entirely agreeable. She knew Priscilla had resented all of the girls who were always after Elvis and even the girls who filled his suites after a show—

although most of them were invited there by the Memphis Mafia. So Linda played it cool. Her thoughts were to never upset Elvis or try to tie him down.

A girl told me: "I think Linda was more like a mother to Elvis—because she was protective of him, always watching out for him, but not trying to fully possess him. Two of the three times I had a date with Elvis, there was Linda with us, making it a threesome. She was entirely congenial so you couldn't object. The only thing was, she and Elvis had a sort of pig-latin vocabulary, a way of putting endings on words so they could talk to each other and no one, unless you had the key words to their system, could understand what they were talking about. They only used it in emergencies when I was along. They'd always laugh and apologize for using it, saying it was top secret, highly confidential. That is why so many people who heard them talking that way thought it was baby talk, or some lingo from Mars or another planet! Linda and Elvis could carry on their conversations in their own code as easily as in English, and no one knew what they were talking about.

"I think Linda was very good for Elvis," said this beauty, who asked to remain anonymous, since she does not want her name ever used in gossip about Elvis whom she loved very much. Elvis gave her a diamond friendship ring, but when their names appeared in the news, she never heard from him again. "I was not trying to exploit him," she said sadly. "I wept when he died.

"I do know that Elvis seemed to respect Linda. I once asked him if he liked the way Linda dressed—because she wore the cutout bikinis. Elvis would laugh and say, 'That's Linda.' But when photos of his ex-wife Priscilla began appearing in the movie magazines, showing her wearing very, very brief clothes, exposing her body, he was angry. He didn't want Priscilla, the mother of Lisa Marie, his daughter, to wear clothes like that.

"Actually at heart, Elvis was old-fashioned. He had the southern gentleman's viewpoint, that his women should be covered up. What they did at home with their own man, alone, away from curious eyes and the public gaze, was another matter. That's what Elvis said one time. He let me go to Susie Cheesecake's boutique in Las Vegas and buy a lot of cute things and charge them to him. 'The bills go to Graceland,' he said. I was to have what I needed and wanted.

"I know some girls ran up big bills on Elvis. Mine was almost $500. Elvis seemed quite unconcerned. 'Did you get everything you wanted' was all he said."

Linda was crazy to be an actress. She made two mistakes with Elvis. She did a lot of redecorating of Graceland and had it photographed. Elvis was livid when he heard about this and responded with an explosion of that quick temper he had. He thought she was going to give the pictures out to a magazine. Linda had to make sure they did not land in print.

Linda began taking trips on her own with her girl friends. One time she went to New York, where a magazine writer cornered her for an interview. This was her second mistake. Linda, with plans for a movie and TV career, gave one. When the interview was printed, it turned out to be all about Elvis. Elvis was very angry. He considered anyone's giving out interviews about him as a complete breach of friendship and trust. Soon after those events, he paid for and furnished an apartment in Hollywood for Linda. He said he'd help her all he could to get a career. She began getting modeling jobs and TV parts.

*   *   *

One morning a girl from Houston, Texas, long-distanced me, asking: "If I come to Hollywood, will you see me? I have a great proposition to make."

Soon after, the girl arrived. She was very pretty—big blue eyes, a tan skin, a length of tawny red hair, and a whistle-stop figure. In a matter of moments, she laid it on the line! "I want to meet Elvis Presley more than anything in the whole world. Since you know Elvis, you can make this possible. I am twenty-one and a half. I've come into my inheritance on my birthday. My daddy has oil, lots of oil wells. When he died last year, I, well, I am his sole heir. Get me to Elvis and I'll pay you $10,000. You don't have to do anything but just get me to him. That's all I want. After you introduce me, you can go. I'll give you a check in advance, or the cash, either way."

I laughed and said that would be impossible. I couldn't accept her proposal.

"All right, this is my dearest wish, and I know you are my only way to meet Elvis. You can take me with you on an interview—say I'm your secretary, anything. I know I have powerful sex appeal and once Elvis sees me, he'll never be able to resist me. Okay, I'll give you $20,000." She finally offered me $50,000 and I do believe, with any encouragement, she'd have gone to $100,000 for me to set up a meeting with Elvis!

I declined all the way. I could never use my friendship with Elvis that way, I told her. First she became very angry, then she wept, then she pleaded. I felt sorry for her but, "no way," I said. "I'll find a way," she flung at me as she left. I never mentioned this to Elvis. I guess such extraordinary offers were par for the course for anyone close to Elvis. Since I quickly forgot about her myself, the next time Elvis and I were together I forgot to mention it.

Perhaps she was lucky and found her own way to meet the man so many millions of girls like her absolutely craved to meet—even just once—and at any cost or price!

6. Playgirls, Prostitutes, and Femme Fans

Once it was known that I knew Elvis Presley, girls began calling me, all kinds of girls—famous stars, starlets, and unknowns, good and bad girls—all offering me stories about Elvis. Always it was an account of their romantic trysts with the super sex symbol. Anything to get their names in the columns, for a name coupled with Elvis's name meant instant fame!

I was always very careful not to write up their fantasies, which I am sure most of them were, in my columns. At first I'd listen in amazement to their tales. But I'd soon cut them off since my time was not like Rudy Vallee's famous theme song, "My Time Is Your Time."

It was well known both in Hollywood and Las Vegas that the boys of the Memphis Mafia were always looking for new faces, new bodies of pretty girls—at least in the beginning. "Good Old Southern Boys," as they called themselves, they were dazzled by the sex appeal and gorgeous looks of the Hollywood feminine contingent. And they went after it all on sight, with a true sense of vocation, whenever they were exposed to it.

As the years went by, it was also often reported that they would approach a likely miss with the come-on invitation, "Would you like to meet Elvis Presley tonight? Come up to his suite and we'll have a party." Nine out of ten girls eagerly agreed. Too often they said that en route upstairs they were propositioned. "First you have to make it with me—so I can see if you are good enough for Elvis." Most of the girls, including several Las Vegas show girls, said they'd do their best to please some of these bodyguards, but still they never got near enough to Elvis in person for even a kiss. "It was peddling what we got for free, with those damn cocky Memphis Mafia," said one.

Here are the accounts of some of the girls whose stories were plausible enough to listen to and worth relating here.

A nice, Sunday-school-going girl, age nineteen, told me the following: "My girl friends and I heard that Elvis Presley played touch football in a small public park in Westwood. We went out there many times before we were lucky and one day, they were all there. It was easy to recognize Elvis. He was the best player and he looked great in his uniform and helmet. All his boys wore the same, but they were dumpy in looks, comparing any one of them to Elvis. Elvis moved with grace and style, giving it his all. We sat there with a hundred others, watching for a couple of hours, until the game broke up. Before we could get to say hello to Elvis, the boys surrounded him, put him in a car, and he was whizzed away.

"We stood there, disappointed, until a couple of Elvis's guys—we knew who they were because they were wearing the same uniforms—came over. Said one, 'Would you like to meet Elvis?' What a question!

" 'Would we?' we gasped in amazement. 'We most certainly would,' I replied.

" 'Okay then, have you got a car?' Yes, we had. 'Then follow our car closely—we are going to Sunset, then up Stone Canyon road and on up to Elvis's house. Follow us.'

"Gleefully, we followed at full speed right behind them. Right on up to a big electric gate that opened and stayed open only long enough for our car to pass through right behind the boys. We learned one was named Joe Esposito. We parked in a space where several expensive cars were parked, and the boys motioned us to follow them inside the big house.

"It was an elegant, tremendous-sized living room. We were invited to have something to eat, make ourselves comfortable. There were big platters of freshly made sandwiches on a big table and chips and dips and all kinds of soft drinks. There was a big chocolate cake that hadn't been cut yet. Within the hour, a lot of other girls and fellows kept arriving until pretty soon, there were as many as fifty in the room. Some played pool. Some watched one of the big color TV sets. My friend Becky and I just sat there and watched. One of the fellows came over and said, 'Would you like to go in and sit in my bedroom for a while?'

" 'No,' I said. He asked Becky the same question and she said, 'No.' He shrugged his shoulders and walked away and ignored us the rest of the evening.

"We were going to see Elvis, so we stayed on and on and on. But Elvis never showed.

"Suddenly, who did we recognize but Tuesday Weld coming in the door all by herself. We had read she was dating Elvis. So we thought now Elvis would be coming out to see her. But he didn't! She sat around like the rest of us, ate some sandwiches and watched TV and didn't talk to anyone. Nor did we.

"This went on all evening. Some of the girls paired off with some of the fellows and disappeared into other rooms of the house. They'd come back looking disheveled and we knew they'd been having sex with some of the fellows. Elvis still did not appear at all. Someone said he was in his suite alone. He had had his supper served in his room and had already gone to sleep, as he had an early call at the studio the next morning.

"When we heard that, we left. So did some of the other girls who'd come alone without dates. Outside, as we waited for the electronic gate to open, a girl volunteered, 'I've been here a few times. I know one of Elvis's boys. You always have to have sex with one of the boys first before he'll even let you meet Elvis. They always will ask you point-blank if you have VD or are you 100 percent clean. I know a couple of hookers who've been here, for I've met them at the VD clinic. They are so mad at the rip-off of these guys, getting them up here for free sex, they are hoping they give them a dose.

"'Honestly,' one of them told Becky and me, 'girls are wasting their time if they expect to make it with Elvis. He doesn't pick up with strange girls. Sometimes he'll come out and talk and be perfectly charming. But he doesn't invite them into his room for a trick or two. Elvis is a real clean guy. He doesn't mess around like his Memphis Mafia. Those guys actually give Elvis a bad reputation, but Elvis is not like them at all.' "

This girl and her friend never did get to meet Elvis, or even see him, they said, except to watch him at a distance playing touch football that one time. They both remained his sincere admirers.

Another woman, who is a petite, curvaceous brunette, a real extrovert, had this to tell: "I'm eighteen. I've been an extra in pictures, and I was lucky enough to work in one of Elvis's pictures, *Wild in the Country*, at 20th Century Fox studios. I made it a point, even though all we extras were told in advance not to try to talk to Elvis, to give Elvis the eye. He looked a bit puzzled at first when I kept staring at him in my most provocative manner. The second time I winked at him, his face broke into that wonderful half grin. From then on, whenever I could I'd get into his eye range and he'd recognize me and start to laugh in a nice way. I knew I had it made if I could just make closer contact. It took a long while. I'd met Max Baer, Jr., who was working in pictures at Warner Brothers. I told Maxie it was my big ambition to meet Elvis. He said the next time he played touch football with Elvis in the park he'd let me know. To keep calling him.

"I kept calling Maxie all right, almost every day in fact, until he finally said, 'Listen, chick, you be at the park tomorrow, late afternoon, and you'll see Elvis. I'll see you get to at least say hello. After that you're on your own!'"

"It worked out just fine. I went to the park and watched the game. Elvis was superb. When he and Maxie and some of the guys stopped to drink Cokes, I dashed right over. Maxie ran interference for me—not letting Elvis's guys chase me off. And I met Elvis. He was as nice and polite as apple pie. He offered me a Coke. I said after a bit, 'I'd love to come to one of your parties up at your house in Bel Air, El.'

"He replied. 'Don't call me El. My name is Elvis.'"

He was a little bit turned off that I had assumed such familiarity by calling him El. Then he said, 'No one who is a friend or who knows me calls me El. It's Elvis.'

" 'Okay, Elvis,' I said. 'I'm sorry.' I rolled my eyes in such a way that Elvis knew I was truly sorry. Then he laughed and said, 'Okay, follow the guys when we leave here, and you can come up to the house. There's usually a hundred people up there on weekend nights like this. You'll at least have something to eat—and you can do whatever you want.'

"What I wanted was to make love to Elvis and Elvis to make love to me, just like in my dreams. But I could see by his attitude that a girl could not come right out and say it like that. You'd have to build up to it. Elvis, I was surprised to learn, was actually shy, even modest. It was hard for me to understand this. Elvis Presley is a superstud sex symbol—what is a girl to expect?

"I'd made it with other famous superstuds. And Elvis seemed so special. His songs got to me and all through me! I had hopes before the night was over he'd be my latest conquest. And maybe, just maybe, I'd get my name in the columns as a new item with him. Would that set me up but big in Hollywood!

"To tell the truth, no one will believe me, but there were so many gorgeous girls already at his house and a lot of guys and other people, like record executives from Elvis's hometown, Memphis, Tennessee. It was plainly an 'open house,' with food, trays of food, coming out of the kitchen like on an assembly line.

"But where was Elvis?

"I walked around and it was like Elvis had just disappeared. I went searching around and opened a door which had to be a bedroom, since it was on that level of a hallway. The bed springs were squeaking like a fire-alarm signal. I saw the two bodies—a fellow with long, blond hair on top of a girl, making it like there was no tomorrow and it sure wasn't Elvis. I closed the door, saying, 'Excuse me for invading your privacy.' Same thing inside another door I opened.

"With such luck I decided to make my way to the kitchen. I simply followed some of the empty trays and found the kitchen. I asked a lady, who was one of Elvis's cooks, where I could find Elvis. She said that his quarters were off limits. That I should go back where I belonged. And if and when Elvis was in the mood to join the party, which would probably be a little later, he maybe might appear. And then again, maybe not. It turned out she and her old man were the couple who kept house for Elvis. And distinctly, she made it clear I was not her type.

"There was nothing to do but wait. Then suddenly the red, plushy paper walls parted! And out stepped Elvis. The walls were electronic wonders. Elvis stood there smiling, looking magnificent in an elegant velvet suit of deep blue studded with rhinestones. Man, he looked magnificent.

"I jumped up and ran right to him. "Are you Moses dividing the Red Sea, coming out this way?' I asked. This pleased Elvis, for he laughed. "You know your Bible, I see," and I didn't tell him I had seen that in a movie. I just said, 'Of course.'

" 'Can I speak to you privately, Elvis?' I asked.

" 'What about?' he asked.

" 'I want so much to make wonderful love to you,' I whispered.

" 'Oh that . . .' He actually blushed. Here, the super sex symbol stud of all time blushed when I suggested sex.

" 'Thank you for the compliment,' he said. 'But thank you, no, I have guests to see.'

"He tried not to hurt my feelings. I give him credit for that. But what a turndown. However, some of his boys were after me the rest of the night. I brushed those louses off but good. For me, it was Elvis or no one. And I didn't score.

"An hour later, Elvis walked toward those red plush walls, they opened, he stepped inside, and presto, he disappeared again. It was like a movie. Then, to my surprise, later on the walls opened and out he stepped again. This time he was wearing an entirely different costume. It was red and white with a huge silver belt and gold tie. Everyone exclaimed, 'Ooh! Ooh!' Elvis was giving us a fashion showing of his new threads.

" 'My tailor is here for fittings. I might as well get everyone's opinion as I try them on,' he declared. Elvis looked magnificent.

" 'Maybe after you're through with your fittings, I could join you inside,' I dared to say, because I was getting very horny—so much I couldn't wait. And I was not going to waste all of myself on those crude old country boys working for him.

"Elvis said, 'Relax,' and right away he vanished behind those walls again. And he didn't come out again.

"The evening was a heartbreak for me. How could he refuse me, I wondered, as I looked at myself in the nude when I got home. No one, no man I'd tried to make it with had ever refused me. Only Elvis. I guessed he had too many girls after him. I realized it wouldn't do me any good to try for him again.

"Somehow I still have that eternal crush on him. He's so polite, so compassionate about my feelings for him. He didn't want to hurt me by turning me down—as he did—oh so gently."

A third woman, this one tall, a redheaded, beauty, announced to me that she was a professional, $100-a-trick hooker. "A lot of Elvis's Memphis Mafia have picked up hookers on the streets in Hollywood," she said, "all promising that if they find them good, they'll give them Elvis. I'm twenty-three and experienced in every trick in the books, and then some besides. I'd decided Elvis Presley was to be mine!"

To my amazement, she took $100 bill out of her purse and said, "Here, this is for you—to make the introduction."

"But I can't," I told her. "I absolutely cannot accept money and I can't introduce you to Elvis Presley!"

"In Vegas his boys take money all of the time—from professionals and even some amateurs, to get up to Elvis's suite for a party. No one knows which girls are pros and which are not. Do I look like a pro?"

"No," I admitted. "I haven't really met any pros that I know of," I said, a bit embarrassed. She had called me, using an articulate, highly educated voice to say she had a scoop news article for me, and she identified herself as a friend of the late Tyrone Power. Of course a friend of the late Tyrone Power would certainly be welcome to my house, as Tyrone was a dear friend.

"You're really square, Miss Mann," she said. "I'll bet you've made it with Elvis!"

I was shocked. "Of course not," I replied, now offended at her presumption. "Neither Elvis nor I are that kind of promiscuous people."

"You mean Elvis is old-fashioned and square like you, too? I don't believe it!"

The woman was now getting very rude. Seeing the look of distaste on my face, she quickly apologized. "I'm sorry. I just thought it would be so easy to meet Elvis through you. But I will make it. You'll see.

"I've got as much as a $1000 bill for making it so good for some of the top men in the business. All men want sex, whether they are Elvis or his grumpy henchmen or his lackeys he surrounds himself with. I have class and I'm particular. I don't let just anyone have sex with me. Why . . . ?" She stopped and laughed. "Am I embarrassing you?"

"Yes," I said. "I never dreamed this would be this kind of an interview."

"Wake up, young lady." She was flip now. "If you get around Elvis Presley, the world's greatest stud, as much as I read about it—and *you* can't get him—obviously you have very little to offer him!"

With that she departed. Since I never heard from her again—thank goodness—I don't know what luck she had. But knowing Elvis, I am sure she was not his type.

In Palm Springs on a weekend vacation, while sunbathing by the hotel pool, I was accosted by a seemingly rather shy young blond. Pointing to my column in a magazine, she declared, "I recognize you! I enjoyed this story you wrote about Elvis Presley. Perhaps you'd like to know about my being at his house last night, here in Palm Springs?"

Then she told me: "Some of Elvis's boys were down here at the hotel yesterday, and they saw a couple of us girls at the bar. They invited us up to Elvis's house for dinner. Naturally we went. We knew it would be a sexy, f——ing good evening. They'd told us that already. Elvis has a four-bedroom and seven-bathroom house—very nice, in fact beautifully furnished with everything you could ever desire. We had a barbecue by the pool. Elvis already had a girl with him. He never said who she was. I think her name was Linda. She was gorgeous in her skimpy bikini and did not mind everyone looking, for her body was really beautiful—tall and terrific.

"After the barbecue all the guys shouted, 'Skinny-dipping time.' Then and there they began taking off their clothes and jumping into the pool. We did too. We looked to see Elvis follow suit with his girl. Instead, they just lay there on their mats, and did not make a move to join us. In fact, Elvis looked embarrassed, and he and his girl got up and went into the house.

"One of his men said, 'Don't mind Elvis. He's a prude. He doesn't like anyone to see him in his birthday suit, not even in the men's showers.'

"That's the truth of how it actually was," she said. "We slept over and got up this morning to a nice breakfast of ham and eggs, served about noon. Elvis and his girl friend joined us. Everyone was very nice. One of the boys called a taxi for us, gave us the money for the cab driver's tip, and we got back to the hotel an hour later. It was some evening. But those Memphis men are big blahs in the hay!"

7. A Famous Star Reveals Her Night of Love with Elvis

During his twenty-two year reign as the King of Rock 'n' Roll, Elvis the super-star sex symbol was exceptionally modest off-stage. "Elvis," I laughingly asked one day, "how does it feel to be the world-renowned and proclaimed sex symbol?"

Gasp! Gasp! Swallow—"Huh?" Elvis's shock turned to devilment. "Wanta find out?"

My turn—gasp, gasp—even though I knew he was only fooling. "I just ask, because all of those thousands of females swooning over you would like to know."

"Well," he decided in the affirmative, "I've never had no complaints!" And we both broke up in laughter. Elvis was never known to discuss women or sex; never!

A year after Elvis's death, a famous star friend said to me, "I'd like to set the record straight on Elvis as a lover. I'm sick of all the make-believe junk about his supposed escapades. Elvis was never promiscuous. He would never touch cheap women or married women, who threw themselves at him. He was very moral and a one-woman man.

"As everyone knows, Elvis and I had known each other, but we had never been physical. It was after his Hilton show one night; his boys were gone and he was lonely. We were eating sandwiches and listening to records in his suite when we both got caught up in the spell of the music. After a while Elvis turned to me and slowly drew me into his arms. It was as though the mood of the music effortlessly carried us into the bedroom. Gently he held me. The smell of his lips, his mouth, his skin was so clean, his arms so strong and vital, yet not forceful.

"'I'd love to love you,' he whispered softly.

"There was no pulling at me, rather just his sheer charisma. We lay in each other's arms on the bed for a long long time, in gentle embrace. His kisses were sweet, at first gentle, then gradually they became feverish and demanding. Slowly he undressed me, so lovingly. He made me feel I was the only woman in the world!

"Nature had not only endowed Elvis with talent and a beautiful body, but with a tremendous physical sex organ—that throbbed with heat and energy, as I believe no woman has ever experienced. His gentleness turned to torrid passion, but with controlled regard for me—ever mindful to please me. He was so romantic in making love. It was sheer ecstasy between us, almost unbearable. When he was certain that I was ready to release him, only then did he release me. We lay there dreamily in each other's arms and fell asleep.

"With daylight he was still so sweet and darling, so

protective of me. He made a call, and then took me down a private stairway to my own room with tenderness and a thrilling kiss, a lingering one, he whispered, 'I want to thank you for such a wonderful night."

"A few hours later, a messenger arrived with a basket of red roses which enclosed a jeweler's box holding a beautiful gold bracelet set with diamonds. A card said, 'I shall always remember.'

"Unlike most Vegas superstar studs, Elvis never collected girls for a quickie and a quick brush-off. He had no taste for kinky sex. What his boys did disgusted him and embarrassed him. It was well known that they'd slip him a tranquilizer so he'd go to bed and sleep—so they could carry out their fantasies with women. Elvis never participated.

"I want the truth known that Elvis was a tender, exciting, and wonderful lover. And he, unlike many stars who keep trays of cheap rings as the quick pay-off for a quick affair—when he gave gifts, they were of quality and the best."

8. How Elvis and I Met

The millions of Elvis's dedicated lovers, whose numbers span four generations, will find this highly unbelievable, if not completely insane. "I don't want to meet Elvis Presley!" I said. "Why would I want to meet a twenty-two-year-old hip-swinging singer who's being banned by the PTA as a bad and vulgar influence on today's youth?" That was my reply in 1956. I now blush to say it—and I certainly never, in all our years of confidential exchanges, ever mentioned that stupid turndown on my part to Elvis.

It was Hal B. Wallis, the eminent Academy Award-winning motion-picture producer who, while he was in New York City for the premiere of his latest film, made me the offer. I was the celebrity columnist on the *New York Herald Tribune,* which along with the *New York Times,* was the most prestigious newspaper in the United States. Why, I asked Mr. Wallis, was he making me this outlandish offer.

"Because," replied Mr. Wallis in a patient manner,

"you will be the only one of the press to ever get to know Elvis Presley. I have him under contract for motion pictures. He has made two on loan-out to 20th Century-Fox. Elvis, you should know, is not only already, and almost overnight, a superstar, a multi-million dollar record seller, the idol of millions of fans. . . . His first two films, in which he stars, have cleaned up millions at the box office. He's the hottest and biggest box-office star this world has known to date!"

"Why me?" I demanded. "I only interview the stars who are my friends, like Clark Gable [who made me his protégée and gave interviews to no one else but me since I first arrived in Hollywood]. And well, really, Mr. Wallis, the *Herald Tribune* and the people who syndicate my column like big, big stars of great prestige."

Mr. Wallis, however, is a very convincing and persuasive speaker and I finally agreed. "If you really think it isn't a waste of time, I'll meet your Elvis Presley—just one time, anyway."

Since I do not wish to repeat the exact sequence of events that I have already told about in my first book on Elvis, but only wish to say what I left unsaid, I'll simply and briefly mention the fact that my first meeting with the real private person, Elvis Presley himself, was the great surprise of my life!

As I read over my notes, and transcripts from my talks with Elvis, I remember the wonderful moments Elvis and I shared and all the beautiful, soulful inner thoughts he gave me the privilege to share. It was an experience to live and relive, and to cherish forever, a treasure few people have known. To make up for the terrible loss, I offer the following chapters with their glimpses into the real, private Elvis, the Elvis I knew and loved, as a memorial to all of the true fans who will only love him more when they hear his own genuine words and as testimony against all the vicious detractors whose books prey on his dead flesh only to feed their authors' bankrolls.

9. Elvis Reveals All of His Illnesses, Including Cancer

One day, only three weeks before Elvis's demise, Bobby Morris was visiting Elvis at Graceland to select new musical arrangements for Elvis's next record session and happened to call me to say: "Elvis is hoping to be well enough to see a little more of the world. He's been so very ill and the cortisone bloats him, which embarrasses the hell out of him. He hates being called fat. Elvis said, 'It is hard to believe this, Bobby, but recently I've been so sick, I had to talk my way through part of the shows, just couldn't make it. And a few people booed me and I announced they could get their money back. I didn't blame those few because they had flown in from Canada, stood outside in a long line in the cold waiting to get in, tipped the maitre d' plenty for a good seat—so they said—and then I could only do a half show. I was very sorry.

" 'I don't want to die yet, before I travel a little,

that isn't working, just being a tourist like so many other people. It is more interesting to have good company with you. Cilla was, when we first went to Hawaii; then Linda was great fun. I took Ginger and her family, but it was not enjoyable.

" 'My daddy scolds me: "They're just using you, Elvis," he says. I spent millions on Cilla and Linda and my daddy liked them. He liked May Mann, and I hope to take her, when I go from California to Australia. She's intelligent and good company.' "

Three weeks later Elvis was dead.

It makes me angry to realize anyone should have to defend Elvis Presley after his death. "After I'm gone, give the rest of my life, May. Outright lies will start the hour I die," he said.

"I've been real sick but I've got to keep up the Elvis image, you know," he said with a wry laugh. "The glamour, the virility, the big macho man—that's what everyone expects of me!

"I don't know sometimes how I can go on, but they give me shots to keep me going. Gotta make that money for them!

"And what is money?" Elvis philosophized. "Money sure doesn't buy me happiness.

"All those girls who really loved me—or was it the kind of sporting life and the diamonds, planes, cars, clothes and big houses? Living like a millionaire always appeals to poor folk. Everyone knows what 'poor folks' the Presleys were, until I took up singing.

"I get pretty deep down into the blues," Elvis confided. "I don't mean just singing. I mean me. I've got Lisa to live for, but some days I feel like turning up my toes to go to rest with my mama."

Elvis was feeling nostalgic during this particular conversation, which took place on the telephone.

Lengthy long-distance calls meant nothing to him. He would often stop for what seemed like long moments, pausing, deliberating, choosing his words carefully. It was *"hold on"* until he felt like talking more.

Usually, he never discussed his health. Now he was letting it all out—how he really felt. "It's boring seeing television, always switching stations. Priscilla left me. My mama's long gone. All the Colonel cares about is keeping me going on the road to keep bringing in the dough-re-me. And I'm getting old. And I look fat!"

"Elvis, come off it. Don't feel so sorry for yourself," I said. "You're only forty-two, that's not old. You'll get rid of this bloat. Rosalind Russell takes cortisone, too, [this interview took place before Ms. Russell's death] and it bloated her up. Once you can stop that kind of medication, you'll slim down again."

"No one talks about me being born with a hereditary degenerative liver disease. You know it killed my mama and my two uncles. It's killing me, too. You can't say that out loud for it spoils the 'Elvis Presley image.' Everybody's got me hooked on drugs, and I'm no dope fiend. Everyone pounds 'drugs'!

"Mama was forty-six when it killed her. Everyone is saying she was forty-two, same age as me. Mama, as I told you a long time ago, liked to be a couple of years younger about her age. That's 'cause she was a couple of years older than my daddy. Remember I told you when she died she was forty-six, her true age. We put it on her tombstone. Everyone's thinking I'll kick the bucket now I'm forty-two. And I probably will."

Since we had known each other and had so many intimate conversations for almost twenty years, Elvis could always talk to me on anything.

"Look, I've got glaucoma. I have to wear glasses. I have a heart-trouble problem—that's probably from taking off weight so fast for the movies, so many times. My kidneys are not good. Since 1967 I've been treated for hypertension, high blood pressure. The worst is this liver disease. And now bone cancer. That's what I carry on my back.

"Sooner or later, no matter how many doctors and hospitals, that will be it."

Elvis, talked out, was laughing now. His sense of humor laughed at his self-pity.

"The Good Lord knows how hard I try to get in physical condition. When you have so many things wrong, where is the strength, where is the energy? The doc is always with me. . . . But the Colonel makes the tour dates, and he keeps me at it."

Then Elvis disclosed, "I want the Good Lord to take me. If it were not for Lisa . . . who else? . . . what else to live for? There's plenty of money in the bank for Vernon, for Grandma and Aunt Delta . . . plenty to keep them in style here at Graceland.

"No, I'm not upset that my daddy has Sandy, his attractive nurse, with him. She's good for him. She takes care of him. My daddy could pass on any day, too."

Vernon's nurse and her children lived with Vernon on the grounds of Graceland. Elvis's mother's suite in the mansion remained locked with all possessions, clothes, mementos, as though she were just away on a visit. A trusted maid was permitted to air and clean it from time to time. Elvis often went there for a few hours of aloneness with "their" memories.

After another long pause, Elvis spoke again. "I have learned all about Jesus Christ and God, especially in these last years of pain and suffering, which has become a daily breathing part of me, physically and mentally. With it, I have read and reread the Bible every day and every night. I have learned all about life and what life will be after death. I am ready to go at any time. But it sorrows me plenty thinking how it will hurt my little girl, Lisa Marie, and my daddy and my grandma. My favorite song and record is 'How Great Thou Art.' I want to fulfill my mission on earth. Whatever it is, I must do—although at times my life is more than it is humanly possible to bear. But it is God's choice, not mine."

Elvis often talked about death. "I won't live longer than my Mama, poor dear darling." He died two days after her birth date, August 14.

When I first met Elvis I asked him if he didn't do a lot of reading of books, when he had to spend so much time confined in his room to avoid the mobs that his immediate presence created, due to his great popularity. Elvis was only twenty-two then. As always, he replied with such amazing honesty. "I never read books," he said. "Should I?"

"Of course you should, Elvis. I read a book a day. I find such pleasure, such knowledge and such an education in them. I'm going to send you *The Prophet*, by Kahlil Gibran. It contains a beautiful philosophy. Now, if I go out and spend three dollars plus tax for it, to give to you, will you be sure and read it?"

Elvis laughed and replied, "I will."

And he did. After this he began reading voraciously and I was continually amazed at the knowledge he had acquired between our visits. Elvis had a very sensitive and brilliant and most retentive mind, all of which qualities are clearly shown in the Christmas letter he wrote to his father and quoted earlier. His movie directors declared Elvis could read a script one time and deliver it letter-perfect.

"Someday you and I are going to spend some time and write something really worthwhile together," he said. Then adding, modestly, "if you will? I keep putting my thoughts into my tape recorders. I have a lot of material, although I don't know whether it is any good or not. When you come to see Graceland, I'll let you hear some of it and you can tell me in all honesty what you think."

I regret that I never got to Graceland on Elvis's invitation. Life and earning a living in Hollywood are such busy and confining enterprises, I just never took the time—and this is a big regret of mine. Elvis always said, "Just let my daddy know, and he'll send you a plane ticket—even if I'm on tour. You've got to see Graceland."

"Elvis, why do you let people use you?" I once asked him. "I'm aware of some of it," he had replied. "People are human. . . . They all want easy money and the good things of life. I have always shared whatever I have with everyone around me. I'm happy to do it. I can imagine, when I couldn't even buy a suit with matching pants and jacket how I would have felt if someone had suddenly said, 'Here son, go in and buy whatever you want. It's all paid for.' As for cars, I remember too well when my daddy and I had our first old jalopy. It would go downhill but we would have to get out and push it uphill. If someone had suddenly come along with, 'Here son, go in and get yourself a Cadillac,' or 'Here's the keys for that new car. It is all paid for,' I think my daddy and I would have fainted. I understand the pleasure of giving and the pleasure of receiving. The Good Lord has blessed me with so much, so much more than I need. And I am only too happy to share and to pass my good fortune on."

At this point, let me repeat what I said in all of the

personal appearances, radio and TV shows I was doing for six months after Elvis's death to set the record straight, that he was not a drug addict, etc., etc. This question always came up, as well as other, more surprising ones. So many people asked: "What was your salary, writing all of these years on Elvis?" or "What kind of money were you paid?" I was amazed. I was not on salary of any kind. I met Elvis and we became friends. I just wrote the truth about him. More recently I have been asked: "How many Cadillacs did Elvis give you?"

The answer is, "None." The idea of payment of any kind never came up in my thoughts, ever. Yet I am still hounded with questions like: "What kind of jewelry did Elvis give you?" Everyone seems to think my fingers should be covered with diamond rings from Elvis. But again, the answer is, "None." I never expected any. I don't think Elvis ever thought of it either. For when we talked, our conversations were never about gifts at all.

However, I must honestly say that toward the end of his life, Elvis did think of giving me something. For he said: "Wait until I see you again. I'm having something made for you special."

"For me, Elvis?" I was taken by surprise.

"Yes," he said. "When I play Vegas, you come up and you will see!"

"What is it?" I was now curious and excited.

"A ring with diamonds; you'll see."

Of course Elvis passed away and never made his last Vegas engagement.

I mention this conversation to offset another kind of remark I often hear. People often say: "All you did for Elvis . . . he never appreciated it and took it for granted."

That was never true. Elvis always thanked me sincerely. He was especially thrilled but totally surprised the day he read that I had written and proposed that he should be President of the United States. Elvis could well have been elected. This story was cover-featured and headlined from coast to coast. Elvis, when he saw me afterward, said, "Oh May . . ." But he smiled with pleasure. His tremendous following and popularity aside, Elvis was known for his honesty and integrity all over America. With the voting age lowered to eighteen and with the solid South behind him, he could easily have been elected President of the United States. There was no more likely candidate at that particular time.

The idea came to me during one of many times I often asked Elvis what in the realm of possibility he would like most in the world. Twice he said, "To go to the White House and visit the President of the United States." This he did, receiving honors from President Nixon.

Elvis was also pleased when he was singled out as one of the most respected and foremost young men in our country and presented with an award.

Elvis once told me, as we talked about what he wanted Lisa Marie to remember most about her father, that he had but one motto to live by. "Always live by the golden rule. I believe it and I have always tried to live it, just as my mama and my daddy taught me as a little boy. 'Do unto others and as you would have done unto you!'"

I will always remember the time Elvis and I talked about death. It was a few years after he lost his mother. It was late afternoon at Goldwyn Studio. I asked Elvis, "Do you believe, as I do, in life after death?"

"Of course," he replied without a moment's hesitation. "It has always been of great comfort to me to read the Bible." And he quoted: "Jesus said, 'Let not your heart be troubled; ye believe in God, believe also in me. In my Father's house are many mansions: if it were not so, I would have told you. I go to prepare a place for you.' John 14: 1–2."

"Elvis, what about all you have worked for and will leave behind you if you should die?"

"I read somewhere," he replied, and he amazed me by his accurate quotation from memory, " 'Of all created comforts, God is the lender; you are the borrower, not the owner.' " Then Elvis reached over with an affectionate pat on my shoulder, and with a smile brightening his face, he jumped up, exclaiming, "Why are we so serious, May? Come, let's send out for a Coke and a sandwich. I don't think we have to worry about death for a long time! Do you?"

Happily, I was caught up in his lighthearted change of mood. It was just that we had these long talks from time to time and I'd ask question after question and we'd cover every subject we could think of. Elvis was slim and trim now—with no hint of any future illness.

"Here, I'll show you a new karate hold," he called out excitedly, and he demonstrated on me . . . until I yelled, "Help . . . let me go!" Then with a light kiss of affection on my cheek, we both walked out of the sound stage to where his black limo with the drawn curtains was waiting.

"Till next time," Elvis said, showing me to my car. Then turning, he walked in the gathering dusk of the evening to his limo, his broad shoulders so erect, with an almost military bearing. Suddenly he turned around, and laughing, he called back, "I knew you were watching me. Go on home before it gets dark."

Which I did.

*   *   *

In going over my notes now from other chats with Elvis, I came across another thought of Elvis's. He had expressed it to me at the time when he was first getting blasted by the ministry as "a bad influence on the youth of America" Elvis told me then, back in 1957: "The kids understand me. I get carried away with the music and the beat. It's not vulgar. It's fun. Like my mama says, and she gets so upset when she reads anything against her son . . . well, mama cut out this poem for me. It goes like this:

'When things are breaking wrong for you,
This is the thing you should do:
Grit your teeth, throw out your chest,
Wipe off your chin, pull down your vest!
Allow nothing bad to ban your way,
Fight harder still to win the day.
Then things are bound to come your way.'

It's very true, isn't it?"

Years later, I recalled this advice in verse from Elvis's mother and looked it up in a volume of poetry. To my surprise Elvis had recited it letter-perfect.

"Even if it looks like you're on top, you've got to keep on trying harder," he said and sighed. "Mama always had something good to turn any dismay I felt at times, and plenty of disappointments, into courage to go on.

"My mama always said, 'Do not be afraid son. Just keep pushing ahead, have faith in the Lord . . . and whatever is good for you, you'll have.' As long as the Good Lord is on my side, I don't have anything to worry about. I have always trusted God in my heart. And I have always acknowledged his guidance and help." Religion was so much a part of Elvis that he was not in the least self-conscious in discussions.

"It is my dream, the Good Lord willing, to repay some of the many blessings he has given me. I want to go on a gospel singing tour . . . a lot of them, and take his message to the people. That is my dream, my big dream. I want to give my time and my singing free, doing his work. I think my daddy will go along with this dream of mine, too. He will help me."

10· Elvis Explains His Frequent Solitude and Confides His Frustrations and Desires

From the time Elvis first came to Hollywood to make films, it was said that he periodically locked himself in his suite at the Hollywood Knickerbocker Hotel, then in the Beverly Wilshire Hotel in Beverly Hills, and finally, in the numerous houses he leased or bought there. The big question on everyone's lips was: "Why does Elvis lock himself up alone for hours, sometimes for days and nights?" Every move Elvis made aroused the curiosity of his coworkers.

Even Joe Esposito, his top henchman, could not break into Elvis's solitude once the door was shut to Elvis's quarters. In case of an emergency, Joe could leave a note slipped under the door. Otherwise, the ultimatum was, "Leave Elvis alone." That was the law!

This went on for a few years before I ever thought to ask Elvis himself to tell me the truth about these self-imposed periods of solitude. When I did so, he replied: "Everyone needs them, don't they? It does not seem so unusual to me." That was all he said.

Then one day I laughingly asked Elvis, "What do you do when you lock yourself out of circulation? I have hundreds of letters from your fans who want to know."

Elvis started to laugh, too. "Is that such a mystery?" he rejoined. "Wanting to have some privacy?"

Then he qualified this remark. "I've always been that way, I guess. I need to be alone to think things out. To make decisions. To ascertain in which direction I am going. Don't we all? You can't concentrate on serious matters or otherwise when you are constantly with other people."

We were interrupted before he could say more, for Elvis was called back into a scene for *The Trouble with Girls* at MGM. "See you later, Elvis," I said, scurrying off for an appointment. I wanted to ask an astrologer about Elvis and learn what and how Elvis's stars impelled him. I also wanted to reassure myself in my own mind because to me, Elvis was extremely brilliant. He had a very good mind. Whenever I'd expound at length about that fact in my columns or magazine pieces, editors would laugh at me. So I sought out a famous astrologer in the hope of gaining deeper insight.

While he was going over Elvis's chart, he said: "Let me tell you, that boy is brilliant; his intellect is that of a thinker. He has a great intellectual capacity."

"Aha," I responded. "I was right. I've always said so and almost no one believes me. They think Elvis is just a singer, with someone else being the brains behind him and pulling the strings, like Elvis Presley is a puppet!" Said this astrologer: "Elvis has that real bearing; you'll note the way he walks, the way he carries himself. His inner modesty at times may make him self-conscious, and he'll tell a joke on himself or pull a prank, but Elvis is dependable and responsible. He has one of the most distinguished charts in the zodiac that I have ever seen. He weighs every word carefully, you'll observe, before he replies. What he says is always worthwhile and realistic.

"You must know he is a born leader and people instinctively react to him and accept what he says without question.

"Elvis has and always will have admirers and fans by the thousands, but unfortunately, few true friends. When he discovers that a friend is not true, and the ones he expects to be loyal and sincere, the ones given so much—when they turn Judas—it plunges Elvis into a deep depression. Sometimes almost despair. He realizes from experience that the only ones he can fully depend on for loyalty are his father and his grandmother. Everyone is out to profit and benefit him.

"Elvis is like the sign of Capricorn the Goat. It will butt it's head against a stone wall, being unrelentlessly determined and headstrong. Elvis will even try to change the unchangeable.

"Elvis has tremendous psychic powers if he develops them. He can discern and see through people when he takes the time to consider them. That accounts for his long periods of solitude, which he needs: First, to restore the tremendous energy he exudes in all he does. In other words, to recharge his batteries. And second, to think things out. He has a quick mind, and he makes snap judgments.

"I must say, unfortunately, there is a lingering illness that will surface in his life. Regretably, it will be a lingering illness inherited from his relatives. He should be more careful of his money and stop throwing it to the undeserving. He should stop taking on all of the obligations of the people around him. It is a big burden and he's such a nice guy, he doesn't know how to say no—to all of those hands reaching out continually to take from him.

"If anyone wants to be Elvis's real friend, he or she must avoid trying to pry into his secret reserves; avoid attempts to force a social life upon him if he prefers his natural taciturnity; and don't try to make him over. If you can't take him as is, better let the whole friendship drop.

"Women should know that the one way to win and hold a Capricorn man is to know that the element of secrecy plays a big part in his life. She can well assume a veil of mystery herself. Even a touch of aloofness intrigues Elvis. Remember he likes to pursue women, rather than be pursued. His love is usually permanent once it is won.

"Elvis is inclined to be moody and introspective. He is always fair-minded, and during any difference of opinion, if an appeal to the practical side of his nature is made to justify one's behavior, he will readily admit any validity without rancor. Elvis is always fair, never unfair."

These words were so in keeping with the Elvis I knew, I was astonished to hear them from someone who did not. I decided I'd tell Elvis everything this man had told me—except the part about a future illness. Why needlessly worry him? After all, Elvis was the picture of radiant, perfect health. In fact, I never saw Elvis sit, completely relaxed. Always, his right foot was tapping, even though he was unaware of it. It was sheer nervous energy.

The astrologer had further revelations to make

about Elvis. "Elvis loves beauty, beautiful music, good books, peace of mind. Respect his moods and the long periods of his soul-seeking thoughtfulness, for he needs to spend much time alone, pondering over people and life; this satisfies the side of his nature which is frustrated in his daily affairs.

"Meet his desire of privacy. Never inflict relatives or friends on him when he is not in the mood. He will resent even well-intentioned interferences from an outsider. His temper can go boom—but he has great patience, and after blowing off steam, he quickly forgets the intrusion.

"He admires women who are witty and who keep up with the world's events. Also, a woman should know when to talk and when to keep quiet. He can be jealous if provoked, but with a child in his marriage, his interest will never actually stray. Nor his love."

Well armed with information after my session, I went back to see Elvis. I read him the notes I had taken—most of them. He smiled when I was finished.

"It's true. That's me all right." He sat down thoughtfully and looked over at my notes.

"Sometimes I'm on a quick diet, to drop twenty pounds before a movie. It is easier for me to stay by myself and diet, even go on a fast for a couple days or so, than to mix with everyone in the family or the boys. Otherwise," he confessed, "then I want to eat the good things, too.

"It's strange how cameras make you look twenty pounds heavier, isn't it?"

Elvis was very slim and trim at this time, as I've mentioned. You'd never have suspected he would ever have to worry about his weight. "I don't worry about my weight," he said, "except those twenty pounds on occasion. On tours, I quickly work it all off. I usually skip lunch on a picture." This time Elvis was on a peach yogurt kick; a 120-calorie cup was lunch. "I get a steak, a small one, and a salad at night. Oh well"—he smiled—"the price of fame is the name of the game.

"Now seriously," he said, "you ask what I do behind closed doors. Does everyone think I'm making some secret inventions or some mysterious chemicals like in *Dr. Jekyll and Mr. Hyde*?" Elvis laughed. "What would I be doing alone? Changing into a rabbit or a devil or a witch and going out the window on a broomstick to fly about the world and frighten people? Come now . . ." Elvis shrugged his shoulders. "Who'd believe that? But it isn't any more ridiculous than some of the manufactured stuff I've read about me!

"I like to read. I have the biggest travel library, photos and histories of almost anyone in the world. If you come up to see me sometime," he quipped àla Mae West, "you'll see dozens of big travel books replete with colored pictures of all the countries in the world, the ones I want to visit and see. And to date, I have not. I did see a little of Paris and a little of Germany when I was in the service, but not very much. I've seen Hawaii a few times, but I'd like more than anything to be free to take off and see the world.

"I'd like to wear dark glasses or some getup that would make me look not like Elvis and spend at least six weeks sight-seeing. I'd like to get on a tourist bus and listen to the guides tell all about each historic place. I'd like to go to China and see the Great Wall; I'd like to visit Singapore; I'd like to go all over England see it's splendor, it's pageantry, visit Carmarthen, the birthplace of the legendary King Arthur's wizard Merlin. I'd enjoy seeing the Hampton Court Palace where King Henry VIII lived and raised the very devil with his wives. I'd like to see it all. Instead my life can become monotonous—movies, tours, home—like a set schedule. Then I start it all over again, the same sameness.

"I'd stop overnight at tiny villages, in the Cotswolds, and in Wiltshire—with it's Castle Combe. I have read all about it. I'd like to stay in little pensions in Italy, not the first-class hotels. I'd like to see the Bay of Naples. I'd like to go to Tahiti! I'd like to go to a Cannes Film Festival, Hong Kong, Paris—so many places I want to see. Here I am, passing time in this world and not seeing it. I'd see the real French countryside, and go to Israel, see the Holy Land. I'd like to go to Egypt. I'd like to go to Holland, see Amsterdam. I'd like to take a cruise ship on the Mediterranean and the Caribbean. I'd love to see the Taj Mahal in India, a bullfight in Spain, or in Mexico. I never get to go anyplace, no travel, except when my tours start again—which are one-nighters and never include any sight-seeing."

Elvis was letting it all hang out—all of his many frustrations. They seemed endless. "I get all the travel folders and read them over and over. Everyone in the world can go—except me. Oh"—he sighed—"it isn't fair. I get so lonely, too, for companionship. Everyone has some one person who is 'in-love' and a real companion. I am so alone at times. I get so restless. I love performing. I sure do. But I want just some of the ordinary things in life, too. Half the time I'm happy to be me. And half the time I wish I were someone else!"

I'd never seen Elvis in this mood before. He had the compulsion to express his true feelings. And I was more than sympathetic to his situation. Being so walled in—not a participant in life—not even a close observer. Always forced to be remote and to view

things from an imprisoned distance. Such self-denial
... what a price he was paying to be Elvis Presley!

"I keep on buying so many books, illustrating and
telling all about the world I want to see and can't. I
keep telling myself, 'You only live once Elvis, see it!'
But how? I'd like to go to Alaska, see Eskimos and
baby seals." He smiled. "I spend hours planning trips
that I never take. It would be great for me to be able
to go about unnoticed. Imagine the fun to share in
fiestas and eat native food at small country inns of
different countries. So far, I have not been able to
devise even one way to do it. Could you tell me how I
can travel without all the hysteria? How could I go?
Just me and one companion? Without causing a commotion which embarrasses me. I can't even go to
Hawaii anymore.

"It's nice to be known and I love people, but no
one will know how I long to also have a little bit of a
private life, like everyone else has and is entitled to.
Except, it seems to me, Colonel Parker's poor boy Elvis can't."

As we sat and talked I felt so very sorry for Elvis.
I showed him pictures of myself taken with the
guards at London's Tower, and on the Nile in Egypt,
and . . .

"Did it cost you very much?" Elvis suddenly asked.

"No," I said, "perhaps a couple of thousand dollars
at the most for four weeks."

"I hope the day will come when I can live my life
like I want to . . . seeing the world instead of always in books." He paused for a moment, then continued. "Back home at Graceland, I like to spend a
few days alone unwinding. I listen to music, to radio,
watch TV. I have a private, monitored TV circuit. I
can watch the fans at the gate."

One of his few enjoyments, he said, which allowed

him to mix with at least a few people, was karate. "I like to go to karate classes and watch." Elvis, being a black belt, was at the top already. Years before he had shown me just how adept he was—with a telephone book. With one quick side flick of his hand, Elvis cut it in two.

"What does it do for you, besides make you a potential killer?" I teased. But Elvis was serious.

"Anyone into karate knows that he cannot ever lose his temper and throw a lethal punch. That's out entirely, even though we practice it to keep in form.

"I started learning karate," Elvis said, "in the service overseas. I was into judo before that.

"When I was first starting out in the singing business, there was always some fresh punk who would want to fight me. After I was into judo and the word got around, I could go along without some eager beaver challenging me. Karate," he said, "gives you the feeling of your own energy. It begins to flow. You feel the air going down your sinuses and into your lungs and through them. You feel vibrations by sheer instinct. You develop an awareness of everything about you. Karate gives you a knowledge of your true self and your outward strengths. You learn to give time to meditation, which I do. I am always glad that I have it. It's more than an art. It's a spirited discipline.

"I think about many things," Elvis said before I left. "I read the Bible for hours. I memorize much of it. I go into my music and dream and plan what and how I'll record next. I keep trying to get an inspiration for a real motion picture, a dramatic one, I hope.

"There are so many things that could make my life more worthwhile. That's why I like to be alone for long periods of time: to contemplate, to think and to enjoy a little privacy. There's no great mystery about it. In a business, where I am surrounded by so many people, all telling me what to do, or waiting for me to tell them what to do—that goes on and on and on—it is pure luxury to be by myself. Just let go and read and enjoy the tranquillity.

"There's no mystery to that, is there?" he asked. Then with a kiss on my cheek and a hug, he said, "See you soon," and Elvis was back before the cameras.

11. Why Elvis Gave His Famed Diamond Medallion Cross to a Little Fan

In late November, 1981, Glenda Boler called me long distance from her home in Monroe, Louisiana. She told me about a medallion cross Elvis had given her back in 1975, one he was photographed wearing in hundreds of his concerts. She said, "My house has recently burned to the ground. I'm in desperate circumstances." She began to cry at this point. "I wondered if I should sell the cross, or what to do. I'd rather die than part with it."

I really had no advice to give her except my sympathy. Obviously, she was "for real", very sincere and entirely believable.

I thought about her. Then, on January 25, 1982, I called her back, having found her number on my calendar notation. Her voice had a ring of authenticity. I asked Glenda to tell me again the story about Elvis Presley's famous medallion. Thousands of people saw Elvis wearing it on his tours and there were hundreds of pictures.

"I have been an Elvis fan since I was ten," she said in her soft southern voice. "When he came to Monroe on tour, I took my five-year-old daughter Rhonda to hear him. We were seated in the second row. He saw my little girl, with her blond curls, and just a few months younger than his own daughter, sitting there. He kneeled down on the stage and said, 'You remind me of my little daughter Lisa Marie. You look so much like her.'

"He had, with my permission, a policewoman guard take her up onto center stage, where he sang a song to her, 'I Can't Help Falling in Love with You.' When concluding the show, as he left the stage, he stopped, leaned down, and handed her the silk scarf he was wearing. The people began pushing up, and one woman grabbed one end of the scarf to take it while I was holding on the other end for dear life. I thought my little girl was going to get choked.

"Out of the corner of his eye, Elvis saw what was happening. He rushed back and his security guards dispersed the pushing crowd, and the woman let go of the scarf. Leaning down, he said to my little girl, 'This is for you. It is something I treasure, and I want you to have it. Always keep it.' He took the medallion on a long gold chain from his neck and handed it down to Rhonda. It is set with green tourmaline stones with a diamond in the center. On the back, it is engraved with the words: 'R. G. 9th month '69.'

"We followed his tours, and I made several trips to Graceland, offering to give it back to Elvis. He always sent word that we were to keep it.

"An appraisal for insurance was set at $2000, and

we put it in the bank for safekeeping. We treasure it more than life itself.

"I told Vernon Presley about it in Baton Rouge," she said, "when Elvis was there on tour. He invited us to have breakfast with him. He said he didn't know what the initials meant, but that Elvis had worn that medallion for a long time, even under his T-shirt. So he knew it was very important, but he wanted Rhonda to keep it forever.

"I even talked with Elvis's estate attorney, Beacher Smith, and he said by all means to keep Elvis's gift: 'We are up to our ears in his estate matters here in Memphis.'

"James Burton, who played for Ricky Nelson's band, joined Elvis in 1969, helping him put his new band together. He was one of his lead guitarists, and he says there was not a finer person than Elvis, and all of that junk and lies written about him is just so much junk for money.

"James, and Joe Esposito, as road manager, are now touring with another rock star. It saddens me and everyone who knew Elvis in Memphis to read the lies written about him. It is all so unfair."

Mrs. Boler told me the people who own the Hickory Lodge on Elvis Presley Boulevard across from Graceland bought Vernon Presley's house on Dolan Street around the corner. Vernon had left so many Elvis momentos in it, they planned on making it a museum. Since the zoning laws wouldn't permit this, they moved into the four-bedroom house Elvis built for his father and are enjoying it.

The stories of Elvis's generosity to fans occasionally come to light, but the millions he gave to charities, to the sick, the poor, to charity foundations, he always kept quiet and never allowed to be publicized. Over and above the gifts of jewelry and cars one reads about, these grants and donations testify to Elvis's caring and charitable heart.

The legend of Elvis Presley will unquestionably go on for generations. He was one of a kind. An original. No idol in world history has made such an impact or left such indelible memories. Nor, sad to say, has any star's passing given rise to so much lying and viciousness on the part of people who will do anything to make a fast buck.

12. Elvis: A Hero in Action When the Devil Interfered

Elvis Presley had that rare gift, a certain quality that went beyond his talent and his electrifying personality and allowed him to be himself and to offer his friendship to any and everyone he met . . . to always have his hand out for support . . . to make the time to greet people on a human down-to-earth level, as one person to another . . . and, whenever he saw people in need, to go to their assistance, often delving into his purse and giving generous help, sharing his good fortune with the unfortunate.

All of this was obvious in his appearance wherever he went, wherever people saw him. Small wonder Elvis was such a unique, phenomenon. I asked Tom Diskin, Colonel Parker's brother-in-law, who worked closely with the Colonel and Elvis, about this special quality. We were watching Elvis filming a movie in Hawaii, and I was amazed at his directness and genuine warmth. "How can he stay so marvelously his natural, unassuming self, without any pretenses, without putting on any airs—just being Elvis, as I first knew him? I know many stars who are wonderful people, but at times, under pressure, they can't cope, and it shows. But never Elvis. It is like his hand is in God's," I marveled.

"That's the secret of being Elvis," Tom replied as we watched Elvis performing before the cameras. "He's always polite and appreciative. There's never been anyone like him, and probably never will be." That was way back in 1961, when Elvis was making *Blue Hawaii*.

I believe the true quality of Elvis was published in a Memphis magazine by his own peers, in his own hometown, on his death. It reads: "The highest tribute you can pay a man is to be pleased by his presence and grieved by his loss. By this standard Memphis has well proved its love for Elvis Presley. This love is easy to understand. Though we seldom saw Elvis on our own stages, he remained more ours than Las Vegas, or say Hollywood. They had the 'hot-right-image,' but it was among us that he burned mostly and unseen, with a softer permanence. When he needed a place to hide his light, to nurture his private life, he came back here to Memphis. We were the first to see that he was more than a boy who shook and moved. Here, in one of our own, was a shaker and a mover. But what we cherished the most of all were the things that made him one of us; things he carried over from the shotgun shack in Tupelo, where he was born, the public housing in Memphis— even as he conquered the whole world.

"One sensed in him—especially when he was young—none of the urbane ulterior motives that moved his nightclub imitators, and little of their Hollywood hypocrisy. There was an innocence in his audacity, honesty in his seductiveness. In his pink Cadillac, his flashy clothes, and his dyed black hair, he willingly revealed more of his true self than the slick pop stars, who sport 'natural Sassoons' and sponsor golf tournaments. What he did, he did as we all do, for fame, fortune and love—but with him it was because it seemed he had to. Call it destiny if you want. Or a calling. Whatever.

"At his best—and even at his most outrageous in the beginning, he seemed to say, 'This is what I am. This is where I come from. Make of me what you will.' And he came from here. No popular pretender would have dared to remain Elvis.

"In him was no big-city bluff—just Bluff City brash. His shy mumbles and downcast eyes, when he faced the interviewers' microphones, were set off against the rich raucous voice and, in the beginning, the insinuating sneer on stage . . . and they spoke to everyone of us who has a soul trying to see behind our reserved public self. He sang us HIS SOUL AMPLIFIED A HUNDRED TIMES in the blinding zero of the spotlight. It was the brazen image that gleamed; but those of us familiar with his roots recognized that the model for the brass had been molded in Mississippi clay.

"Here was a man who could have had the world. But he chose Memphis. Not for its skyline. Nor for its tourist attractions. Nor for its money or its prestige. He chose Memphis because this was his home, and he found no other home he desired. This is no time for self-congratulations, but we have a right to be flattered that he chose us. And so much as we are flattered, his own hometown people, so much is that a tribute to him.

"It is hard not to make this sound sentimental, but the sentiment is honest; Memphis, where he was at home, in his mother's house, became after a while a kind of substitute mother to Elvis. She coddled him, she comforted him, she took pride in him. And now, in his death, she feels a mother's grief. That may not be cool. It may not be sophisticated, but it is the truth." This tribute appeared in a Memphis magazine—a revealing, honest one from Elvis's own hometown people.

Elvis was always for the lonely at heart. For them he sang his ballads, his touching love songs. Elvis was always for those who revered God. For them, he sang his spiritual and gospel hymns. Elvis was always for those who were meek and could not defend themselves. For them, he was quick to come to their rescue. It is said by chiefs of police in Los Angeles, in Memphis, and other parts of the country that Elvis often showed up to help a young teenager in trouble and in jail. And this included members of his own family. Elvis would often appear to bail youths out of jail, give them a lecture, first hard and realistic, and then filled with comfort: "I'm sure you won't do anything like this again," he would say.

Quick to defend anyone in need, not only with his money, which he gave a thousand times over—at benefits, giving huge sums without publicity to charities, paying hospital bills, getting wheelchairs, and medical attention for many needy, who praise him for his goodness—but also with his physical strength.

A lady in Los Angeles tells of being mugged on the street, when two youths accosted her, knocked her down to the sidewalk, and tried to take her purse. Suddenly a car stopped with screeching brakes. Out jumped Elvis Presley. He took the two youngsters by the scruff of their necks, bumped their heads together, and said, "Apologize. Help the lady up. Now scram before you land in jail!"

Helping the woman, he realized she had a broken arm. He took off his shirt, bound up her arm, carried her into his car, and drove to the nearest hospital. There he handed her over to the emergency-room staff and told them to send him the bills. As he left he said, "Little mother, you are in good hands. Don't worry. It's all taken care of."

"Praise Elvis and God for sending him to me in my hour of such terror and need," she says.

Another incident of this kind was reported in the Madison, Wisconsin, newspapers: Elvis had appeared in concert in the Dade County Coliseum (capacity 11,000) in October 1976. Due to the thousands turned away he returned for the June 24, 1977 concert there. His limousine was coming in and was only minutes from the airport, where he had arrived from his Des Moines concert that night. Elvis was still in costume, a blue jump suit. It was around one A.M. En route Elvis spotted a seventeen-year-old service-station attendant being beaten up by two older men. Elvis yelled, "Do you see those guys? Stop!" Leaping out of his limousine, he ran up to the three, ready to fight, and yelling as he ran, "Stop it! I'll take you on!"

Forgetting their disagreement, the startled men turned around. Immediately they recognized Elvis Presley, and the fight ended right there. "What's it all about?" Elvis asked, after asking the younger boy if he was hurt. It seemed one of the assailants had been fired by the service-station owner. The younger boy was the son of the owner. Elvis had them talk it over until tempers cooled. "Now is everything settled?" he asked. "Then shake hands." They did.

As Elvis climbed back into the car, the men ran after him. "Gee whiz, Mr. Presley, we forgot to ask you for your autograph. Nobody will believe you did this!" Elvis obliged, and everyone shook hands all around in high, good spirits. There are probably hundreds more of such incidents about Elvis's honesty and bravery and care for the welfare of others.

13. Elvis's Temper Tantrums

In all the years I knew Elvis, never once did I see him act irrationally or lose his temper. But I have heard of a time when he did and fortunately was able to discuss this event with him before he died.

In Las Vegas one night, Elvis, after his show, went to the Flamingo to play blackjack. As he entered the hotel, three drunken men, near Elvis's age, were waiting for him outside. Elvis had slipped out without his bodyguards since it was three A.M., so he was quite alone. The three ganged up on him, muttering "Now, you big sissy. Let's see what kind of a he-man you are, you white-livered lover boy!" It was a terrible moment when they held him on all sides and started to lead him into a darkened corner, saying they were going to beat the stuffing out of him.

Fortunately, a couple came out of the hotel and saw what was happening, although they did not know Elvis was the victim. The woman screamed, the man yelled "Help! Help! Help! in the hope of calling attention to the scene. At the sound of his voice, the drunken bums in sudden fear loosened their hold. Elvis, quick as a flash, went into karate moves and flattened all three to the ground. Instead of moving in for the kill, and kicking their faces to a pulp, as he could so easily have done and had enough provocation to do, he simply brushed himself off. Then, turning to the dazed alcoholics who were trying to get themselves up off the ground, he said coolly, "Next time, you cowards, don't make it three to one. I'm always ready for one at a time."

It was that night back in his hotel room, as he went over in his mind the details of this occurrence, that a full realization of why he had been a potential victim suddenly descended on him and he knew with a terrible certainty that he, Elvis Presley, was a prisoner of his fame—and always would be. To vent his mounting, impulsive, exploding frustration, he simply took a gun and shot out the chandeliers of his room. His fury now released, he called downstairs and said, "There's a broken chandelier up here. Assess its value in the morning and put it on my bill."

"The only other time I let my frustrations get the best of my temper," Elvis acknowledged to me, and he actually blushed and laughed, "was well, when the boys had been taking advantage of me too many times—and began ignoring what I had to say. I simply picked up my gun and fired one shot right into a TV. Man, did they stand at attention and listen to what I had to say! They'd pulled so many tricks on me for money and women, using my name, to get them, I had to make it dead serious. I was serious and wouldn't put up with them anymore . . . until they stopped it."

14. Elvis's Questions-and-Answers Legacy

The following questions and the answers to them were taken from conversations between Elvis and myself. We had so many long, intimate talks during our private times together over the years. I trusted Elvis. He trusted me. How rare it was for him to find someone he could pour out the troubles of his greatly tortured heart to, someone who wasn't out to hurt him.

And so, for the world to hear, here is the intimate record. This private record of Elvis's inner self sings out every time I hear his music. I want you to hear that "record," too.

Q: Is it true that you were called a "red-neck" and hated the South?

A: I am a southern boy and proud of it. I always go straight back to Memphis the minute I'm through working. Only time I was ever called a red-neck, I flipped the guy over . . . took up judo and then karate. I never had any trouble with hecklers. I can talk southern, but for my movies I studied English diction with a dedication in order to play various roles.

Q: Did you change religions from time to time?

A: I've studied all religions. I find good in all of them. I have had many ministers visit me and explain their gospels. I was born into the Assembly of God Church, and there I have always remained.

Q: Rumors have it that you became a Jew when you were circumcized.

A: I've never been circumcized—and I was never a Jew. I like Jewish people. I like all people.

Q: Is it true that Linda Thompson acted like a mama nurse to you for those five years you were together?

A: Linda was and is a great friend. When I was very ill, she nursed me when I came home from the hospital—the trouble I had with my twisted spastic colon. We laughed about putting a pad on my bed like a diaper for a few days, just in case. Luckily, it was never needed.

Q: When Priscilla left you for that karate guy, were you heartbroken?

A: I wanted to get my hands on him and kill him . . . was my first reaction. That's natural indignation. My anger cooled, and I forgave them. Priscilla is the mother of our child, Lisa Marie, and I will always be her friend.

Q: Did you resent having to give her millions in a settlement and all of that?

A: That was taken care of by lawyers and soon forgotten.

Q: When you were named King of Rock 'n' Roll, did it make you feel royal wearing that crown that once belonged to Clark Gable, and you became his successor?

A: I said no one was king except Jesus Christ. When the Beatles first came to see me, on their initial concert date in Hollywood, they enthusiastically called me "the King." So does Tom Jones. I laugh with actual embarrassment.

Q: Do you use profanity in the company of men because it makes you let off steam in a more masculine, macho, way?

A: Never. I have a great distaste for swear words, which my daddy and my mama never used, nor allowed. Nor did I ever hear them in our home.

Q: Do you consider yourself a natural-born genius as a musician?

A: I don't claim to be a genius . . . but, through God's help, I have always felt music inside of me. I began studying and practicing until I could play lead guitar, and I play the piano pretty good. I have always had charge of all of my recording arrangements and chosen my numbers and songs. God has been very good to me, as we have been very lucky and never had a loser.

Q: Are you or were you ever a homosexual? Or AC-DC, bisexual, or did you like sex with both sexes?

A: Good Lord, no. The homos sicken me. Any display of kinky unnatural sex embarrasses me. I won't join the skinny-dippers when they have nude parties in the pool . . . even at my own home. There's something sacred about the body—and especially the reproductive organs—that God created for the purpose of bringing new souls into the world. If Priscilla hadn't left me, I had hoped to have at least a half-dozen more kids . . . and especially a son.

Q: What about those girls that claim they had a baby by you?

A: On investigation they were all dreaming. I would never deny a child of my own blood . . .

but no proof has ever come forward to be real, although tests were made when some tried to take me to court . . . for the publicity.

Q: Are you a voyeur who likes to fantasize and watch other people acting out kinky sex?

A: It disgusts me. Some of the boys brought prostitutes up to the house when I lived on Mondale in Beverly Hills . . . and without my knowledge. They put on a show and invited me to see it. I walked in and took one look, walked out, and slammed the door. I called the culprits in and laid down the law. "You could have had us all put in jail for this. Get them out immediately and never let it happen again!" I was in a rage . . . for them to endanger me and my career with such a stunt. Later, a fink said they had a secret camera and took a picture of me when I walked in . . . to hold as blackmail. I was never able to get anyone to come up with such a picture. If such a one would be found, it would be a paste-up job. That kind of junk, porno films, disgusts me.

Q: Are you a pervert in any way?

A: I am a good all-American southern boy with simple, natural, healthy, wholesome tastes, as my mama and daddy brought me up to be. My music and my songs tell anyone I love beauty and the beauty of romance and of the soul. Anything vulgar repulses me as obscene . . . and I hate obscenity.

Q: Do you have a terrible quick temper?

A: When you have to be locked up most of the time like me, whether it is in hotel rooms or a home—because you can't go outside and mingle with the general public without causing a riot—the frustration of being a prisoner builds up. And when you can't depend on the people you hire to do some of the simplest things for you, go shopping, etc., the frustrations build. One time I was so aggravated I had to explode. I shot a hole in a TV set. This was the most drastic thing I could do . . . to impress and let everyone know I had had it up to here, and beyond, and my impatience with their lackadaisical ways. Immediately afterward I felt foolish for letting my temper take over like that. It almost never happens.

Q: Your directors, David Weisbart, Norman Taurog, Freddie de Cordova, and producer Hal Wallis, and so many others, have always marveled at your brilliant quick, retentive mind. You would take a script home and overnight come back with the whole thing memorized letter-perfect; not only your own lines, but everyone else's. And you also knew each piece of business and action. They've said you are a genius and an intellectual in the raw.

A: Thank you. Since you gave me the Kahlil Gibran's *The Prophet,* I constantly read books. I have read all of the biographies, philosophies, histories, religions, I can get my hands on. I have memorized Webster's giant dictionary. If that helps being intellectual . . . maybe I am. I wanted very much to enroll in college or take night courses. I was turned down at UCLA. They politely said my presence would disrupt classes and the fans would be all over the campus waiting to catch up with me.

Q: You still keep that 1957 pink Cadillac, the first car you gave your mama. You keep it in excellent running condition. Why?

A: Because it is my mama's car, and when Lisa is eighteen I have promised it to her. She loves it.

Q: You have so many honors, Elvis, and all of those gold and platinum multimillion-dollar record sellers in your music room. What will happen to them someday?

A: I hope, if Lisa wants to, when she is eighteen, if she doesn't choose to live here at Graceland as her home, that she will put them into a museum. All of my stuff, despite so much I have given away, will still be here and will be waiting for her. I'd like to share it with my fans. There's a whole new generation of twelve-year-olds now and twenty-year-olds on up. I still get a lot of handmade afghans, sweaters and socks from so many who are grandmothers. They tell me in letters they feel like I belong to them. They all keep up with my records, bless them.

Q: How do you feel about people criticizing your furnishings at Graceland as garish and in bad taste?

A: People can have their own opinions. My mama designed and worked beyond her strength to furnish Graceland. We had so much fun looking in magazines, visiting the big luxury hotels where I worked . . . saw the movie sets where we got our ideas for plush furnitures and mirrors and luxurious carpets, and all the rest. We loved it and I love it. I never have changed a thing here, unless some carpets or drapes were worn out. Of course, when Lisa Marie was born, we had the nursery and her suite built opening into mine. She can walk in anytime and be with her daddy.

Q: Did you have lots of trouble with some of your boys who were on drugs, who worked for you?

A: Plenty. I had them getting dried out and getting them out of jail a lot of times. I don't want to talk about them. They are all trying to leave that stuff alone, they swear to me.

Q: The fans want to build a memorial to you in Memphis or Tupelo. What would you like? They are the little working girls, the older working girls, who have been with you since the start of your career, and the twelve-year-olds and the grandmothers . . .

who all love your music and bombard you with gifts and all of the love notes. What could they give you?

A: I've thought about that from their letters. I think it would be very nice if they would like to build a chapel on my home grounds in Tupelo, which is now a public park. A chapel with stained-glass windows, where they could go and meditate, and even get married. [Note: The chapel, seating fifty people, with stained-glass windows, was built on a hill in back of the shanty in which Elvis was born. It was completed three years after Elvis's death by the fans, who raised over $100,000. for it. Many couples are married there.]

Q: Has anyone built a statue of you anywhere as the King?

A: Not seriously. I'm not "the King" though I appreciate the appellation as fun. I've heard they've been trying to put up a statue of me down on Beale Street. There's an Elvis Presley Foundation with all kinds of plans. [Note: An eighteen-foot sculptured statue of Elvis with his guitar, a very good likeness, stands on a square on Beale Street today.]

Q: Elvis, what has made you proudest besides being the biggest-selling record star in the history of the world?

A: Giving my mama a few luxuries before she died so early and too young. Then, going to the White House and visiting the President of the United States, and being honored with so many sheriff's badges in various states. And reading where my contribution to rock 'n' roll music established me, Elvis Presley, with the same acclaim as the world-acknowledged pioneer geniuses and contributors, to go down in history. It is hard for me to believe all this. Besides, college professors send me congratulations, that's a fact!

Then there's my basement room with trophies inscribed like "To the Father of Rock 'n' Roll whose music has captured the whole world." This is all like a dream and I'll wake up and go back to driving a truck. I can't take it all too serious . . . who could?

Q: How did you feel being approached by national politicians and also Los Angeles city politicians, when the headline came out in 1974 on the cover of a national magazine: "Elvis Presley for President"? Your name has been repeatedly written on ballots all through the sixties. Loved by both black and whites, with the majority voting age in this country under thirty, no wonder the politicians were looking at a sure vote-getter for Vice-President of the United States.

A: I'm an entertainer. But I did love the respect. I read about not being just a rock idol, for they said I had an impeccable character, honesty, integrity, guts, and leadership. My mama would have been proud.

Q: What did you think, being singled out as one of the twenty-one most outstanding men in this country for a national chamber-of-commerce convention, along with Ted Kennedy and other remarkable young men in the news?

A: It was a happy occasion. Again I thought first of how happy my mama would have been to be there with me to receive the trophy.

Q: How did you create rock 'n' roll?

A: Since I was two years old with my daddy and my mama, we'd sing in church in Tupelo. As I grew older I'd sing along with records; then at age twelve I'd twang away on my $12 guitar. Some of my black friends invited me down to Beale Street. This was a real eye-opener. Those dudes were sharp, man, the way they dressed! They'd get me up on stage and I'd sing and twang a tune. Everyone would get to clapping and swaying and singing along with me, with the beat of the music. And I began swaying and swinging . . . which was rocking-chair blues with shoulder movements. I'd start slicking back my hair, had a duck-tail cut to be different, to make me a personality. In a pink shirt and black trousers . . . on Beale Street I got recognition.

Q: Are you a mama's boy?

A: Not in any sense of being a sissy. I loved my mama, but she'd give me a whopping if I was ever late getting home; enough to blister the seat of my pants many a time! I'd come back home as a kid fresh out of the old swimming hole. And mama would have a washtub full of hot water and make me take another bath anyway. I always shower in the morning and again before dinner. And when working, I get so sweaty in those vinyl jump suits, I like two more showers. I can certainly qualify for one thing: "I'm a clean kid!" I swore when I saw my mama, sick and in pain, scrubbing floors in a hospital, and I saw the swell ladies drive up in their Cadillacs, I promised myself that some way I'd make enough money so she wouldn't have to work when she had so much pain in her. And when we could afford a doctor and prescriptions, she'd also have a Cadillac to drive. A pink one, too: making my mama's life easier was my entire goal.

Q: Were you pals as you grew older?

A: Mama was my encouragement to make something of me more than being a truck driver. She was afraid of those knifings and muggings down on Beale Street. And if I didn't get home by a certain hour, I'd sure telephone her. Then it became a habit . . . she wouldn't go to sleep until she heard from me. No matter where I was, I'd call her and say good night.

Q: How do you think of sex? Natural? Sophisticated? Funky or repulsive?

A: Like the romantic songs I sing; to me nothing is more beautiful or exciting than real love between a man and a woman . . . like my daddy and my mama had. They had real love and never were unfaithful. As a child we lived in a two-room shanty. Sometimes I could hear through the thin clapboard wall my daddy making love to my mama, saying such beautiful things to her. When I innocently asked her about it, she told me the facts of nature, in such a beautiful way I never had to hear it first from the street-wise kids. I hold it as sacred. I never talk about my romances, for whatever they are, they are sacred, and just between me and the lady.

Q: You've had several love affairs, without marriage, except to Priscilla. How do you feel morally about them? Do you play around?

A: I always feel that Priscilla is my wife. That is a great heartbreak I have never fully recovered from. I am not promiscuous. One lady at a time has my heart, or affection. I have never taken a married woman . . . that would be adultery. I obey the Ten Commandments to the best of my ability. I know I will meet my maker and my mama when I get to heaven. I fully expect to get there. The Good Lord knows I have had more temptation that most men can stand, but I have been able to abstain from any cheap kind. When I have followed my human biological urge, I pray about it. I'm sure God, who is the creator of us all, understands. Any girl I have enjoyed a relationship with has always had her parents' approval and given me the same. And the friendship was never broken, when the romance was over.

Q: How do you feel about your acknowledged imitators?

A: The Beatles and Tom Jones became my friends. I showed them all I know and we've had some great jam sessions at my homes together. They also liked the real southern dinners I gave them: fried chicken, hominy grits, black-eyed peas, country gravy, mashed potatoes, honey and biscuits, and sweet-potato pie.

Q: Did you ever feel you were cranking out songs and movies too fast, due to the popular demand?

A: I never cranked out records. My time between recordings was given to selecting and trying out hundreds of songs and arrangements to find the right one to record. As for my films, they were formula movies. They all made big money at the box office, and I never saw the scripts until the Colonel, who never read them, except to get me a contract, gave his okay; a million and a half dollars, plus the music rights for each one. I finally stopped. I was tired of the formula. Until my afflictive illness prevented it, my goal was to become a good actor; I aimed to shoot for an Academy Award. The different directors encouraged me so very much. They told me I had the natural talent and incentive. I believe I could have done it with a great script, had I kept my health. I've always been eager and determined to be the best, to win my goals . . . until my health has been holding me back. I get very discouraged. Sometimes I'm so sick, I feel like I'm just enduring . . . marking time . . . until the end.

Q: Your detractors state facts on you as though they were proven truth. How do you feel about all of that?

A: Since the Colonel made it a rule and a law to me to never give interviews, no matter what was said or written, I never objected, since I was not allowed to see the press. But when they said I was on drugs . . . that did it! I spoke out onstage at the Vegas Hilton in 1974. I was furious. That put a stop to that drug rumor.

Q: What about one story that you got kicks out of homosexual and lesbian sex shows.

A: Kinky sex disgusts me. Some of my boys like skinny-dipping parties at my swimming pool in Palm Springs. I never attend. They have brought dirty movies home to run. When I see them coming up on the projector, I am embarrassed. I leave the room. I am an all he-male. But raw toilet sex repels me completely.

Q: Is that fat terribly hard to get rid of, and doesn't it embarrass you to come out onstage . . . when you were always so slim, with the perfect body of the sex symbol?

A: It is very embarrassing. It is the cortisone for my liver disease, and it puffs you up in the stomach, neck, and face . . . as it does all people who have to take it for this illness. Without it, I'd soon die.

Q: What do you think of the critics who are unfair to you?

A: God knows that I always do my best . . . and if I can, I try and work as hard as my strength allows. The first time I ever had a pill of any kind was in the army in Germany. Sometimes during those long overnight, toughening training marches, someone would give you an upper to keep you going. Then you got so high you'd have to get a downer to sleep. I never cottoned to that unless it was necessary to do it. *I've never been a dope taker or fiend, never.* Only doctors' prescriptions for my different illnesses. And the Good Lord knows I have more of those than any human can bear.

Q: Are you a true musician born with the talent to make music?

A: I like to think so. I am on my own at all times with my recordings. The Colonel never has a say. I supervise the arrangements, I play lead guitar and the piano, anything you ask for . . . learning it by ear, and then sheet music after I was twenty-two and could afford a piano. In the last few years, I am into gospel religious music, and those are my favorite albums. If I had my way, I'd go entirely into the Lord's work and music on tours.

Q: The critics acclaim your music as real music, even though a lot of it is rock 'n' roll music. Does that make you happy?

A: Yes.

Q: Elvis, you've always been a leader, never a follower. The Beatles, the Rolling Stones, Tom Jones, they all pay tribute to you starting it all, and happily admit they copy you. Does this make you happy?

A: Yes.

Q: Did you ever sleep with your mama?

A: Are you kidding? My daddy slept with my mama. You aren't crazy enough to suggest incest? No, of course not. Where did you hear such a crazy thing as that?

Q: How many records have you sold, Elvis? [Note: This was 1977.]

A: At last count, five hundred million.

Q: No one in the world, Elvis, even came close to that. Why do you think your records outsold every singer in world history?

A: People liked them. I was astounded to first read that I was named the Father of Rock 'n' Roll and would be known as one of the stars of the fifties, along with, imagine, President Eisenhower of the United States and Queen Elizabeth of England. The national poll referred to me as "the King." Imagine that?

Q: At the start in 1957, in one year, your records and souvenirs and paid admissions added up to $120 million. After that, it has always been twenty and thirty million a year. How does it feel to be so rich?

A: I don't know, I never think about it. I can have cars and give them to my friends who need them and help a lot of people.

Q: Did you ever consider yourself a hysteria raiser, what with your fans screaming. Sex shimmers from you and envelopes everyone who is caught up in it grasping and holding on until the buildup finds release in screams.

A: No, they just get carried away with the music and the beat, like I do. I laugh at it all, me and my gyrations. It's a put-on. Then everyone relaxes. They've had a good healthy exercise. It's an emotional and physical release . . . not vulgar.

Q: How did the drug rumors start?

A: When I've been so sick I couldn't go onstage for the second show, I was given a shot to get the strength to do the show.

Q: Is it true you constantly take pills?

A: If any one person had all of the sickness I have, they'd be doing the same thing. It is all by prescription for my five illnesses . . . which no one knows I have, except Dr. Nick. He's on a big salary and travels with me to keep me going.

Q: What made your act so unique?

A: Colonel Parker set me up to it . . . saying, "Elvis, when you sing rock 'n' roll with the music like you do . . . did you ever see a woman shimmy dancer?" He took me to see a movie with Gilda Gray doing the shimmy from head to toe. Man, I practiced that shimmy dance until I had it down pat. That's what I did . . . it fit the music and when the music played, I followed my inclinations and went right with it. And so did the kids.

Q: What are you doing right this very day?

In Las Vegas, Elvis and I posed for what turned out to be our last picture together, a short while before his death. Elvis's illness had only just begun to show on him. It was a happy time. (*May Mann*)

Elvis close-up. His charismatic smile captivated everyone. (*Wide World Photos*)

After Elvis's death in August 1977, crowds of admirers poured through the Music Gate outside of Graceland to pay homage to their beloved idol. (*Wide World Photos*)

Elvis and I on location. We had spent the afternoon talking about his mother's death. That accounts for the pensive expression on Elvis's face. (*May Mann*)

I visited Elvis on location in northern California. In this photo he is showing the James Dean sneer he was advised to use in all photographs. But once the shot was taken, he laughed and gave me a hug and a kiss. *(May Mann)*

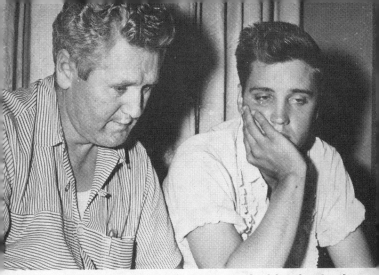

Elvis and his father Vernon were crushed by the death of Gladys Presley. Elvis had flown home from Fort Hood, Texas, on emergency furlough to be with her in the hospital. (*Wide World Photos*)

To the end of his life, Elvis thought of Graceland as his mother's home. (*Wide World Photos*)

Elvis and Priscilla pose proudly with their newborn daughter, Lisa Marie, in 1968. (*Wide World Photos*)

Elvis loved entertaining and gave his all to his audiences. He said, "It's a love affair—me and all of them listening out there." (*Wide World Photos*)

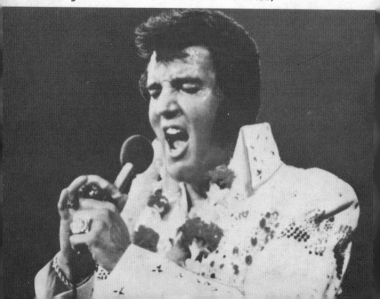

This is Elvis early in his career, singing at a county fair. The sweetness of his personality comes across so well in this photo. (*Wide World Photos*)

Sgt. Elvis Presley, U.S. Army. Elvis was offered a soft job as an entertainer, but he refused. (*Wide World Photos*)

Elvis's birthplace in Tupelo, Mississippi, and the Elvis Presley Memorial Chapel, which stands beside it. Elvis's father, uncle, and grandfather built the house in 1934. Since 1979 people have visited the chapel from all over to marry or renew their wedding vows. (*Photos courtesy of Janelle McComb*)

A: Right now I'm readying to leave on tour, and Lisa has been here with me these past three weeks. She's always bursting in with, "Daddy, can we do this?" and, "Daddy, can we do that?" We leave tomorrow. I have to go to the dentist tonight. I'm taking Lisa on the tour. I've introduced her a few times by having her stand up for a bow. Then we douse the lights and I have her quickly carried backstage . . . in a hurry. Afraid of kidnappers and those threats.

Q: Elvis, who will take your place someday?

A: Lisa could take my place any day. She sings . . . she sings just like me, only better, and she's only nine. She's been practicing with my records ever since she was four. She's a great little mimic. While I'd like Lisa to go to college, and get an education I never had—except reading lots of books—if she wants to be a star, she is ready. Lisa just walked in now. She's asking if we can get a soda and drive out to the airport to our plane, the *Lisa Marie*. She loves to play house in it and have a picnic.

15. I Named Elvis "The King" After Clark Gable's Death

From 1974, to 1977, the press was giving Elvis a rough time of it in print, constantly saying how he was "fat and forty and over the hill." I was naturally very upset. So was Elvis, because there was little he could do about his water-retention problem, which caused his heretofore sleek, sexy body to become somewhat bloated, and he had to sustain an image of himself as the world's number-one sex symbol. But his fans and the public at large loved him anyway and often proved their love by setting all-sold-out house records wherever he appeared.

But the press, who had always been prevented from interviewing him, even speaking to him all these years, was highly indignant and angry. They had no power over Elvis nor the Colonel. Colonel Parker simply would not let them get to Elvis. There had been no scandals, nothing they could use to get even. So they made up stories, for the public demand for news of Elvis was constant.

Now at last, when Elvis began looking fat, they had their revenge. And how sweet it was! In 1973, when Elvis wore velvet suits, beautiful fur-trimmed costumes, and hats and jewels in his private life—looking like a royal prince—any pictures any photographer was lucky enough to grab were used over and over again. They were also made into composites, setting the scene in many different places, turning the negatives around to make them appear like new Elvis photos. After all, the press had a job to do.

There was no one to say Elvis was very ill, that he was bloated with cortisone for his hereditary, degenerative liver disease, that he had a water-retention problem that made his face and neck and stomach puff up while his arms, legs, and hips remained normal. Cortisone, any medic can tell you, can bloat anyone up to forty or fifty pounds above their normal weight in a few days. Yet it was necessary to administer these drugs to Elvis to keep him alive—all the while that his disease was slowly killing him.

Elvis had never had a press agent. He had abided by the Colonel's edict: "leave them guessing, no matter what is said about you Elvis, or at what costs. That's good show biz."

Meanwhile I'd continually plead: "Elvis, please stop working. Go to a hospital until you are well . . . even if it takes years or whatever."

Elvis would shrug his shoulders. Of course he was terribly upset about the weight problem, but he was adamant about continuing to perform. "Anything I can do to maintain the symbol of the image my fans expect, I'll do."

Often, before a picture or a tour, he was known to take off twenty pounds in two weeks. This is understandable, given how the movie cameras make a person look twenty pounds heavier than he really is, and all actors are requested to keep underweight. But Elvis, the super sex symbol to four generations, was deeply troubled by his increasing weight. Without the medication, he could not keep on going. Yet with the medication, his weight increased more than he could bear. Either way he was trapped. And then—as if life hadn't been cruel enough already—the vicious attacks of the press began.

I believe, and there are many others who sensed it from his attitude and from the things he said, that he expected death. He knew that he would not recover. When Elvis celebrated his fortieth birthday, he fully believed that his turn was next. There was no turning back the dread disease.

There had never been any serious scandal connected with Elvis's name or image, in spite of the few lies and made-up stories that had been written about him. Only the paternity suit filed in 1970 by a highly emotional, imaginative young woman. No one believed it. She claimed to have been with him on an opening night in Las Vegas when Elvis had his wife, Priscilla, and his whole family with him as his guests. Elvis was declared entirely innocent. Even though similar suits have been pressed by imaginative women, Cary Grant, Clark Gable, and almost any superstar being their favorite targets, Elvis was upset.

As I remember the Elvis of 1969 and the Vegas opening, and then later the cortisone-bloated picture Elvis presented at his fortieth birthday when he was beset by premonitions of death—the contrast is enough to break my heart. Elvis was in such a happy mood back in those days. He had been making pictures in Hollywood for the last thirteen years. Now, with this engagement at the International, he was facing a live audience for the first time in all those years. It brought him back face-to-face with his public. Would he be a bust? Only two members of the press—one was lucky me—were invited to that opening, and it was indeed a memorable, star-studded occasion. I had a front seat and trained my opera glasses on Elvis's eyes as he walked onstage. He was scared—it was written all over his face. He was so slim, after a stress diet, so healthy, so virile and so handsome that everyone gasped when they laid eyes on him. Then he started to sing. Once he had modestly acknowledged the standing ovation given him after his first song, the fears disappeared and I could tell he was *in* and was his old, happy self again.

Chartered planes of fans flew in from all over the world to hear Elvis. He was indeed the king of all he surveyed, and had the confidence and bearing royalty should have, but he was never, throughout it all, "big-headed."

Elvis had been called "King of Rock 'n' Roll," but the title had never caught on. I had been Clark Gable's protégée since I first arrived in Hollywood at the age of sixteen with the ambition of becoming a columnist, and Clark was known from Maine to California and all the world over as "the King of Motion Pictures." It was the Gable title absolute. But Clark had died in 1960, nine long years ago, and I began to wonder if his true successor had not indeed arrived. And if so, wasn't it about time for him to be crowned?

Almost ten years after I got this inspiration, Etta Cortez, the publisher of *Fabulous Las Vegas* newspaper, reported on her front page how Elvis won the title, "King," a title that grew with him and was his until his death. And still is his. There has been no

successor to Elvis worthy of being named "King." He
was one of a kind. Elvis told me, "I'm proud you
named me, but there's only one who is 'the King.'
That's Jesus Christ!"

Etta Cortez wrote the following in her editorial
column, "That's for Sure," on September 1, 1977:

"It was November 16, 1960, and our Hollywood
columnist May Mann sat on a dais in the Beverly Hilton Hotel, surrounded by fourteen superstars, headed
by Sammy Davis, Jr. The audience, packed with distinguished members of Filmsville, USA, paid homage
to MM for her unrelenting dedication to charity.

"At the conclusion of her testimonial, MM
gathered up a bouquet of flowers and sped off to a
nearby hospital, to visit the ailing Clark Gable.
Forty-five minutes later, the King of Hollywood
played his final curtain.

"Gable had taken this young cub columnist under
his aegis when she arrived in Hollywood, giving her
exclusive interviews and his coveted friendship. Now
that he was gone, MM was forced to name his successor.

"It didn't take her long to decide on the charismatic ELVIS. And it was MM who bestowed the title
the King on Presley in her column which appeared in
the *Fabulous Las Vegas* magazine. It spread like wild-
fire.

"MM devoted eighteen years to the writing of her
book on Elvis, spending much time with the singer in
Hollywood, Hawaii, and Las Vegas. When Elvis read
her book on his life last year, he endorsed it, even
though "you revealed too many personal details of
my life."

"It is the only authentic book ever written on Elvis
and he wanted to play himself in the screen version.

(Collectors are now paying over $100 per copy.) Elvis admitted the constant tours were tiring and he was eager to do the film and settle in one place for a while. Unfortunately it is one of the few desires Elvis never realized."

No matter what happened or what befell Elvis, he always showed a smiling, cheerful self to me. His sense of humor was at times very boyish and brought a lot of laughs.

I remember once on Elvis's birthday, he was rehearsing for his first show. The hotel had made a great big chocolate birthday cake for him, complete with candles. Elvis loved chocolate cake, and as he, his entourage, and anyone else who was lucky enough to be there stood around it admiringly while all the candles were lit, Elvis made his wish. He asked Joe Esposito of the Memphis Mafia, his helper, to blow out the candles.

As Joe leaned over to fulfill this request, Elvis pushed his face right into this huge cake, and it was very, very funny in a slapstick sort of way, like a Charlie Chaplin movie. Everybody just broke up. Elvis had that type of humor. And, I might add, even though the cake had been "nosed," everyone ate generous helpings, including Elvis.

16. Elvis at MGM and on "The Ed Sullivan Show"

Howard Strickling, vice-president and director of publicity at Metro-Goldwyn-Mayer studios, called in his staff of some thirty ace publicists to announce that Elvis Presley would be coming to the studio to make a picture. It would be *Jailhouse Rock*. The year was 1956-57.

"No one was too impressed," recalls Esmé Chandler, a top Hollywood publicist then on Mr. Strickling's staff. "In fact, few of us knew much about this new rock 'n roll singer except that we read where ministers and the PTA were trying to get him banned, saying his music and his hip swivels were not only vulgar but were setting American youth in the path of immorality and sexual destruction.

"MGM was *the* big prestigious film studio in Hollywood. We had the biggest superstars in the business. So *who* exactly was Elvis Presley to get *us* excited? Mr. Strickling said he was going to be a very big star, and we were to go all out on a top-grade-A publicity plan. In fact we were to contact all major writers, wire services, and all important TV and radio, as well as all important news media! We all went to work on the Presley project as directed.

"Several departmental meetings with Mr. Strickling were held, putting forth every effort to make this one of the biggest publicity campaigns in the business. When all was in readiness, Colonel Parker and Elvis Presley arrived at the studio.

"Some of us had the unique privilege, which we discovered later was a very rare one, to meet Elvis for a few seconds. No questions, only an acknowledgment and he was whisked away.

"At an appointment with Colonel Parker we presented the list of top names of the press who had all agreed to start the big publicity ball rolling for Elvis Presley with scheduled interviews. We were a little proud of this achievement for a newcomer. The Colonel looked at all of the names, several hundred, including foreign press. We had pulled out all stops in our publicity machine as Mr. Strickling had instructed. The press had all agreed and appointments were already set up for the following several weeks of filming.

"Colonel Parker looked over the lists, switched his cigar to the other side of his mouth, and said most respectfully, 'I appreciate all of your work and efforts for my boy. Now these writers can have an interview with Elvis for five hundred dollars each. Some of the fancier ones should give us a thousand.'

" 'You mean the interviewers are to pay to talk to Elvis?'

" 'That's right. I don't aim to have my boy do anything for nothing. His time is too valuable. We never give it away. That's what I'm here for, to see he gets paid!'

"Well, everyone in the Publicity Department went into immediate shock! You wined and dined the press, wrote advance copy at their request, sent limousines to deliver them to the studio, sent them on extravagant trips, first class, all paid for by the studio, on movie locations—just everything was done by the Publicity Department to keep perfect relations with the news media! And here was Colonel Parker with a comparative newcomer to the movies, and the Colonel was asking us to ask the press to pay $500 to $1,000 for the privilege of speaking to Elvis?

"It was unheard of!

"Howard Strickling was immediately called. He, too, was aghast! 'I'm sure the Colonel was joking,' he said, trying to hide his irritation at this highly unheard of turn of affairs. 'I'll get it all straightened out with him in a hurry. He just doesn't know the film business and the need for publicity to sell pictures.'

"A few hours later Mr. Strickling, still in a state of highly indignant irritation, returned and called a conference of his entire Publicity Department. He acknowledged that the Colonel had stood firm. We would have to call off any press. Seeing Elvis, talking to Elvis, or even going on Elvis's set to watch by any of us was verboten. It was unbelievable!"

Colonel Parker later explained his bizarre demand by saying he didn't want Elvis to be overexposed. His formula was to keep people guessing about Elvis, just as they did about Garbo. Since he had arranged such fantastic contracts for Elvis and had turned this unknown southern boy into a millionaire in the very first year of his career, no one could quarrel with the affable Colonel. In fact, Mr. Strickling and the Colonel, once they had come to an understanding with each other on the Elvis matter, became very good friends. "It is my patriotic duty to make my boy Elvis a multimillionaire," declared Colonel Parker.

During the filming of the picture at MGM hundreds of girls appeared from nowhere and hung around outside the studio gate. They never bothered to make, or apparently even considered making, an autograph request to some of the then most popular box-office stars on the MGM lot—some of whom tested their popularity by pausing at the gate to give the fans a chance to make their autograph requests, all to no avail. These obviously dedicated Elvis fans only wanted to see one star—Elvis—to ask for his autograph. Everyone else was small fry to them, as one explained.

Socially speaking, Elvis was nonexistent at the studio. No one ever saw him around. The Elvis sets were always closed. The studio press agent assigned to the picture was not allowed to say more than good morning to its star. Never was he to ask Elvis any questions. To make up for this deficit, an occasional interview would be arranged with one of Elvis's leading ladies. The result usually turned out to be "the usual mush."

It was at this time that Elvis began his famous habit of giving away cars. When he discovered that some of his very young leading ladies, very young actresses, had to take a bus to the studio, he would surprise them with the keys to a new Ford or some other small car. He also was known to send flowers to the dressing room of his leading lady on the first day of the picture. But that was as far as it went. No matter how many invitations he received to "Come home with me; Mother wants you to come for dinner," Elvis always politely declined.

One of the MGM PR men recalls, "Elvis was very

polite, in fact every inch a gentleman. His mother had done a good job raising him. He was also completely natural, and a very nice young person. He spent all of his time in his dressing room alone, or with his hired boys from Memphis. They would play touch football together during the lunch breaks.

"Only one time did Elvis come into the MGM commissary. Of course the Memphis boys were all with him. We were appalled at the type of rough, rather uncouth-looking boys working for Elvis. They seemed like eager beavers to get everything they could from Elvis and everyone else. Some of them were not past taking bribes to get to Elvis on the set or at his hotel, we heard. We wondered whatever Elvis Presley had in common with these young men who were in no way like him—even though he gave them fine clothes to wear and everything. They lacked polish and refinement which Elvis had plenty of.

"Elvis had a sensuality, when he wanted to turn it on, that could make any and every word he spoke, or sang in a song, mean anything he wanted it to mean. He was sexy, even when he wasn't singing, but in a more polite manner. When he turned it on—it was 150 degrees!"

The Colonel's 50 percent of his client's earnings also made him a millionaire beyond his own fondest dreams, not to mention Elvis's, who could hardly believe it would last very long. Together the pair went on to become an incredible legend.

Elvis appeared on "The Ed Sullivan Show" on September 9, 1956, and set a new record in the Nielsen rating for that already popular show. In the wake of that appearance, a wave of Elvis souvenirs flooded the market, all of which added a few million dollars more to his bank account. Everything from ties, shirts, lipsticks, wallets, jewelry, bracelets of real gold, and Elvis photos in color were avidly bought. Boys all over the country began greasing their hair slick and wearing duck tails, blue suede shoes, and ultratight pants.

During one of my appearances to set the record straight on Elvis, a nice lady from Oakland, California, declared she had an unusual story to tell me about the wild days following the first Sullivan show.

"I answered my telephone one afternoon in late 1956 to hear a nice, well-mannered voice say, 'Ma'am, this is Elvis Presley calling. I hope you don't mind this intrusion.'

"I was speechless for a moment. 'Is this really you, Elvis?' It was shortly after his first appearance on the Ed Sullivan Show. My daughters had been electrified seeing him on Sullivan.

"'Yes, ma'am,' he replied politely, 'I am calling you from my home, Graceland, in Memphis, ma'am. I am taking a survey and would like, if you don't mind, to ask you a question?'

"Of course I didn't mind. I replied in all but hysteria, 'But you should be talking to my three teenage daughters. They'll kill themselves when they hear you called on our telephone and they were not here to answer. Can you call back or can you wait until I get hold of them?'

"Elvis said, 'No, ma'am, I'd rather talk to you. You see I'm trying to take this survey to find out if my appearance on Mr. Sullivan's show was objectionable in any way? Some of the clergy say it was. I assure you, ma'am, I have no intention of being vulgar. That hurt my mama very much. In fact, my mama has cried because she doesn't think her son is vulgar. Will you honestly tell me what you think?'

"'I saw your show with all of our family crowded around our television set,' I replied, trying to catch my breath from the sheer excitement of an actual telephone call from Elvis Presley in person. '*We* just loved every minute of it!'

" 'Would you like to see me on television again?' he asked.

" 'We sure would,' I replied.

" 'Well, I thank you very much, ma'am,' Elvis said. 'My mama will also be very happy to hear that, since it is coming from another mama. Thank you again and give my best wishes to all of your daughters. I hope they will see my movies. I'm in the movies now,' he announced.

"I assured him: 'Elvis, we sure will see your movies. We already have all of your records to date.' I could hardly know what to say, and he—Elvis—was saying good-bye.

"A minute later two of my girls walked in from school. When I told them I had just hung up from Elvis Presley, they couldn't believe me. When they realized it was true, they started to sob. One grabbed the telephone and tried to connect with wherever Elvis had called from. To this day, even though my three girls are grown women, they talk about Elvis calling our home and talking to me . . . and they weren't home. Of course we, the whole family, were and are great fans of Elvis Presley.

"It was a problem for Elvis at the start even though the Sullivan show cut below his waist so as not to allow his hip wiggles to be shown. Soon after that show almost every boy in high school was twanging a cheap guitar and wiggling his hips. As Elvis said later on his concert tour in Oakland, California, 'If I had done what some of these guys are doing on television today, I'd have been arrested!'

"When Elvis's mama died of a liver ailment, we sent flowers and letters to Elvis to help ease his pain.

We never expected replies, for he was already in the service doing his hitch. But to our surprise, we did receive a thank-you note from Graceland. We treasure this more than if it had been a thousand-pound note from the Bank of England."

As it was for the nice lady in Oakland, so it was with the many thousands who worshipped "the new idol" and grew to love him more and more strongly. And just as love grew in the loving, so hate grew in the hateful, a hate that fed on their inability to reach him. Among the latter were a few members of the press and media, who razzed him and demeaned him since he was inaccessible to them, in the isolation of his heavily guarded fortress homes both in Hollywood, when he was making films, or in Memphis, when he was not filming. No matter what some of the media wrote, there were no scandals about Elvis. He remained a good, clean-cut, wholesome boy, who had established rock 'n roll for his generation and for generations to come. Even his most avid detractors, like Hedda Hopper and even Louella Parsons, who tried to decry him since they could not interview him, finally conceded that he was, after all, one of the biggest box-office stars in the world of entertainment.

Even his army record was highly commendable, Elvis having chosen to be a hard-working private when he could have had it easy and been in Special Services as an entertainer. Yet here, however, the Colonel had his say. He told the army brass: "My boy gets paid when he sings." Elvis did not sing until he was once more a civilian. . . . Except, of course, in his shower.

17. One Man's View of his Friend Elvis

Forest Duke's column headlined: "Elvis Has New Hit Because of Bobby." Several months back, Elvis Presley and Colonel Tom Parker had asked Bobby Morris to help coordinate the swivel-hipped singer's 1969 Hotel International debut. Bobby was enthusiastic about a song called "Suspicious Minds." Elvis was just as enthusiastic after he heard the song and decided to use it in his show.

"RCA execs had all of Elvis's numbers waxed at Bill Porter's United Recording Studios," Duke's column continues, "and they were so impressed with 'Suspicious Minds,' they immediately released it as a single. And within a few weeks it zoomed to Number 1 on all the best-seller charts.

"Elvis and the Colonel are so pleased with the Morris music, they've inked Bobby for all future appearances; the next four weeks being set for the International, beginning January 26.

"Bobby was requested by Elvis to assemble an orchestra and become his conductor. Bobby, a featured drummer with name bands, has been a conductor as well for Barbra Streisand and some of the biggest names in show business. The Colonel had known Bobby for fifteen years and, knowing his work and talent, felt Bobby and Elvis would go for each other. They did.

"Said the critics, 'The fantastic combination of Morris's "animalistic" conducting and Presley's "earthy" vocalizing formed the magic of Elvis's album, "Presley Live at the International." ' "

As Bobby tells it:

"When Colonel Parker first invited me to join Elvis, I flew into Hollywood and was greeted at the airport by a big black limousine, and whisked to MGM studios where a luncheon was being given in my honor by the top executives of MGM. At the end of the luncheon Elvis and Colonel Parker were there. Elvis was very jovial and had some very funny, interesting little stories to tell. He was definitely the center of conversation. After the luncheon I was taken on a tour of MGM studios where Elvis had made some of his top movies and went into a huge room full of his gold records and plaques . . . it was truly a magnificent sight. At the end of that I was taken to Elvis's home, again in a big black limousine, where there were two hundred young fans in the front of the gate, and upon entering I was greeted by Priscilla. It was very pleasant, because she was so cordial and very hospitable. After the initial cordiality and a few drinks, we proceeded to listen to hundreds of tunes to distinguish which ones we would do for our opening show at the International Hotel. Some of the tunes which excited me greatly (and which we ended up using) were: 'Suspicious Minds,' 'In the Ghetto,' 'Sweet Caroline,' and 'Memories.' Every time I got excited over a tune, Elvis would set it apart from the others until we weeded out all the choice songs. This went on for days and weeks of rehearsing, staging, producing, and setting the initial show which eventually created history.

"At the opening at the International Hotel, the general atmosphere was one of tremendous excitement and magnetism. The great feeling in the air was beyond words. The show went off fantastically well and everyone in the show including the Sweet Inspirations, Sammy Shore, the Imperials, and myself and my orchestra had so much enthusiasm, like I have never quite experienced again in my career. It was infectious to the audience, and consequently history was made.

"Elvis never finished a show that he didn't come to me and say, 'Thank you, Bobby,' and shake my hand. He had an open way of showing his affection that touched your heart. Sometimes after the show, he'd invite me up to his suite and we'd sit and vocalize around the piano. Usually he preferred gospel songs and love ballads.

"It was very inconvenient to be Elvis Presley. I remember whenever we'd try to go out late at night, it was never take a good elevator and walk through the lobby and out the front door. Instead, we had to go down a back service elevator and through the basement after using another back elevator and stairway from his penthouse suite. Elvis's suite was a five-bedroom, luxury, presidential suite.

"Elvis liked to come to my dressing room, to get away from his own dressing room, where people would hang around all night. They bugged him, but he was too nice to show it.

"I suddenly found all the girls bombarding me—girls, girls, girls—with 'Please, please, introduce me to

Elvis.' They'd do anything, and I mean *anything at all*, to get to Elvis. They knew from the stage that I was with Elvis, and my life became almost as hectic as Elvis's life with their constant demands and desperation to get to him.

"I'd tell Elvis about some of the girls. He'd just smile. He was very gallant and no matter how many offered their bodies, he never put them down or made uncomplimentary remarks about a woman. He was a real gentleman to the manor born. No matter how shocking, Elvis, who remained old-fashioned in his morals and ideals, would make no comments on women that could demean them. Elvis was never gossipy. But he was a good listener.

"Sometimes he did say, 'Bobby, if you see anyone—really nice—a really nice girl . . . bring her backstage. I'd like to meet her.' Elvis was lonely, actually lonely most of the time.

"Elvis was a very intelligent man who liked an intelligent girl.

"He invited me to his Palm Springs house. It had four bedrooms and seven baths, which were always full with Elvis's boys and their friends—mostly girls. Elvis had a housekeeper who was on duty the year round. Meals could be ordered at all hours. There must have been twenty girls and only eight of us men for that particular weekend. Elvis spent most of his time upstairs by himself until about dinner time when he'd come down. Some of the guys and girls skinny-dipped. But not Elvis. Elvis might watch for a little while, but he showed he was embarrassed. He had a charming and rare sense of modesty that was not offensive to the others who did not have this rare quality.

"Every party was always informal in Elvis's suite or at his various homes. You would always find real southern hospitality. There'd be trays of sandwiches, lots of seafood platters with jumbo shrimp, and great sweets and desserts. Elvis never partook of the sweets. After seeing that everyone was having a good time, he'd disappear into his own quarters and his own privacy.

"I last saw Elvis a couple of months before he died. He had invited me to Graceland. We spent several days going over music and plans for his next recording session. We had a mutual respect and friendship which involved a great deal for both of us. And usually at any of Elvis's gatherings, it would wind up with gospel singing around the piano and telling stories.

"It seems impossible that he is gone. I remember Elvis well. What a great, generous man he was . . . and his kindness and compassion for so many, even for those he knew were using him shamefully. They thought they were getting away with it. But he knew. I heard Vernon tell him he was being used. Elvis simply said, without anger, 'I know, but I know their needs. I remember when we had nothing material'—then he paused—'but we had everything important, Daddy—real love and Mama. I still have my daddy and I pray every night before I go to sleep he'll get well and stay well and enjoy life.'

"Elvis was on cortisone and he couldn't stop using it—doctor's orders—for his illness. I know he fully knew he wasn't going to be with us much longer. He once said, 'I've done what I had to do; the things I wanted to do, I can't do.' I truthfully believed he was ready to go whenever the Good Lord called him. He was at peace with himself and with all around him. Even though those who had hurt him the most by writing an offensive book at the end . . . he did not hold a grudge against them. He only felt sorry for them, to do what they had done. 'I'm glad it is on their conscience, not mine,' he said in a kindly way.

"What a man it takes, to be able to forgive deliberate hurts from those you have loved and trusted.

"I've never forgotten when May and Elvis, by chance one night at the International, met after the show. Sammy Shore, the comedian on the show, had sent May a note to come up to his dressing room after the show. When Elvis heard May was there he rushed in, grabbed her up in his arms, and kissed her. We were about to take some snapshots and Elvis willingly, yes happily, got into the picture with us. Well, next morning there was a big to-do, because May is a columnist and in Elvis's contract he wasn't supposed to see anyone from the press or talk to them. But Elvis said, 'May is a friend . . . the most honest and sincere friend I have. I will always see May, anytime she wants to see me. And I'll always pose for pictures with her. That is my pleasure.' "

18. Behind the Iron Curtain: Brutal Beatings for Listening to Elvis

"Elvis," I said to him back in 1969, "as the Father of Rock 'n' Roll, and its inventor and creator, you will go down in world history and be showered with accolades as the original music genius of the twentieth century!"

Elvis raised his eyebrows in pure astonishment. Then he laughed, partly with disbelief. This humble side of Elvis, which never quite believed how great he was, was one of his God-given charms, attested to by everyone who knew Elvis in person.

"You really think so?" he responded.

"Elvis," I said, "look at all of your acknowledged imitators, thousands of them who sing and twang guitars, copy your jump suits and your manners. Look at even Donny Osmond and the Osmond brothers, David Cassidy, Shaun Cassidy—you name them, they all copy your rock sound, your gyrations and your jump-suit, jewel-studded costumes. Look at the Beatles and Tom Jones and the Rolling Stones, who all acknowledge that it all started with you!"

It was this sensual, wild, vibrating sound, new and undisciplined, composed of the rhythms of black, country, and blues music, which Elvis had combined and unified and turned into his own sound, rock 'n' roll. They all tried to copy Elvis and become instant millionaires. They all widely acknowledged the origin, source, inspiration, and cause of it all.

I wrote about Elvis's genius in my column, "Going Hollywood," and subsequently in a national magazine, and then in my first book on Elvis. "Simply bursting with pride and excitement for Elvis's phenomenal success, it suddenly hit me: the amazing truth: 'Without a doubt your creation of Rock 'n' Roll music, which has engaged the whole world, will establish Elvis Presley with the same acclaim as the world's acknowledged pioneer geniuses and contributors to this generation. As the Father of Rock 'n' Roll, you have to be acclaimed and go down in history right along with Edward Teller, father of the H-bomb; Enrico Fermi, father of the A-bomb; John Steinbeck, Nobel Prize winner for Literature; Pope John XXIII, winner of the Balazan Peace Prize; Samuel Eliot Morison, American historian; John Glenn, astronaut; Neil Armstrong, who first set foot on the moon; Dr. Jonas Salk, scientist—all outstanding pioneers, who have contributed "their thing" to benefit the human race and mankind.' "

Elvis, as was clear from the way his eyebrows rose at my declaration—I shall never forget how he looked at that moment—was disbelieving.

"Oh, Elvis." I was impatient. "An entire world has embraced your creation of rock 'n' roll. How can you question it? It is there. It has to be recognized in world history for the impact it made—is still making. I am right."

"May, baby, you are sweet, a darling," Elvis replied. "Anyway, thank you for thinking so."

"Facts are facts," I insisted. "When the world encyclopedias of your decades—and note I say decades—are written, they will have to state all of that, for your music captured the whole world."

Elvis's return to live audiences in August 1969 at the Hotel International brought special chartered planeloads of Japanese, Germans, English, Canadians, and thousands of fans from all across the world and the Americas. The critics now had to admit, even the ones who had earlier dismissed Elvis and rock 'n' roll, that, "It looks like Elvis the King will go on as the uncontested champion. He has broken every attendance and box-office record of a performer in world history. In four weeks in Las Vegas, he drew a staggering 101,500 persons at $15 minimum . . . a previously unheard of record of attendance for a hotel nightclub. The receipts added up to one and a half million dollars for the engagement. He continues repeating this fantastic success wherever he plays. In fact no advance publicity is given or printed. By word of mouth, all Elvis concerts are sold out within the first three hours after the box office opens."

Elvis and the Colonel were an unbeatable combination.

I have a feeling somehow, as I put down the facts of Elvis since his passing, that somewhere up there he is almost directing people to come to me, or in some manner influencing or directing all of those who have written to me about him. Almost daily, letters come seemingly from out of the blue to tell me of people's personal experiences with Elvis Presley.

A recent and most interesting letter arrived from a well-established author and screen playwright. Its writer reported: "When I was a little boy in Rumania, I was excited about hearing a black-market record that had been smuggled into our Communist, behind-the-iron-curtain country. A record of Elvis Presley's. We youngsters did not know quite what to make of this new sound. Except we reacted to it, dancing around like the most uninhibited. Our parents were not only shocked at our behavior but frightened. To have such a record, which was banned by the Communist government, was not only against the law, but we could all go to jail for possessing it. Communist jails are pretty severe. By the time I was twelve or thirteen, around 1969, we had many Elvis records. All were smuggled in from other countries. It was discovered that I owned Elvis records by the secret police. One summer night they heard the sounds coming through a window which had been carelessly left open. I was given a severe beating. I was really beat up. But it didn't stop me from being an Elvis fan.

"Some of our friends who were older, like seventeen and eighteen, served a few months in jail for being in a crowd listening to Elvis records. They were beaten and half starved. They came out of jail looking like mere ghosts of their former selves. Even so, they couldn't resist listening whenever they found themselves in any group where Elvis records were playing. The police confiscated any Elvis records or material about him whenever they found it.

"Many of us longed to know about Elvis by 1970 . . . but we were only able to get a scrap of information here or there.

"Finally I escaped from the terrible life of living in a Communist country and came to America, where I am a refugee. I have been able to do well here with my writing. Since my family and close friends are still there in my old country, please do not divulge my correct name. Even now in 1978, I fear reprisals should my whereabouts become known. Although the country seems to be freer than it was in my youth, which I say because I know that your book on Elvis found its way there, I am still afraid to send anything about Elvis, for fear of getting my relatives into trouble."

I told this Rumanian fan that the government of Russia had called me all of that long distance when Elvis died—to inquire about his death! It was my impression—even though Elvis had long ago told me that his records were only sold on the black market in East Germany, Poland, and other Communist countries—that he did receive fan mail from these countries—smuggled out. He said, "I only wish that the time will come when I can go to them and sing for them," (In 1978 Elvis records were gathered up and sent behind the iron curtain countries on tapes.)

I have had people stop me on the street and tell me similar stories. A headwaiter at a Las Vegas hotel told me he was from East Germany. He confided: "We were lucky back in the sixties, because when any of us could go over to West Germany, we'd smuggle Elvis Presley records and some of the magazines with your columns and features about Elvis. There was always the danger of being caught. Those who were, those poor kids, were put in jail.

"I was lucky. I got through with my contraband. You should see how worn those articles of yours on Elvis Presley became as they were passed around to hundreds to read. We put them under plastic and treasured each word. We all had such a curiosity to learn about Elvis. There was no way to know more about him until, fortunately, some of the pieces you wrote were found in West Germany."

"What so fascinated you about Elvis Presley?" I asked these refugees. Their answers were always the same: "His music and then reading about what a nice, unspoiled guy he was. And how generous and kind he was. He became our idol."

Said a casino man in Reno: "I have had the pleasure to meet Elvis during one of his engagements here. Instead of giving the big, mighty superstar treatment as some do, he took the time to talk to me and to listen to me. I came away with an autographed picture and a TCB gold Elvis pin. I sent these to my family behind the iron curtain, knowing how thrilled they would be. Unfortunately the mail over there is still censored, and they never received my gifts. I presume some Russian soldier took them and passed them on to his girl friend."

19. Elvis Tells About the Death of His Mother and Talks About Graceland: "Why It Will Always Be Home"

"Elvis Mansion Filled with Tasteless Junk"

"Elvis's Furniture Flashy and Tacky"

"Cheap Ornaments and Carnival Statues Filled Elvis's Home"

These were some of the headlines that were smeared across the pages of newspapers and magazines at the time when the inventory of Elvis's estate was filed in probate court. It is a sad spectacle to behold such cruel and disgusting behavior on the part of writers who persist, after a great star's death, in getting their revenge because of their own failure to hobnob with him, get close to him, or even be invited to pay a brief visit to his magnificent Memphis home, Graceland.

Did everyone expect Elvis to have a house filled with Rembrandts, Picassos, and other examples of the kind of expensive art most superstars collect purely for the satisfaction of their own egos and the craving for ostentatious display that sudden riches beget? Did they think he'd have big libraries of books, all first editions and all carefully placed for maximum effect, though their pages never show a sign of ever being touched? Fortunately, Elvis did not allow those opportunists who attach themselves to "the new rich" and persuade them to buy antiques and objets d'art—thousands of dollars worth—to make them appear sophisticated, elegant, and on a high plane of culture, to fill their pocketbooks by giving him phony advice.

Elvis was for real. His fame kept him from visiting museums, libraries, and other places of high culture where he might have acquired a taste for the luxury of possessing collectors' items. But Elvis possessed a natural gift for interior décor, and he knew what he liked. And what Elvis liked, and the furnishings in his Memphis mansion, is actually quite similar to what you see in many of the stars' homes in Beverly Hills, Hollywood, and Bel Air, homes that were done by professional decorators. So why pick on Elvis, who loved Graceland, who was comfortable there, and enjoyed himself there? And small wonder that he did. It is a true palace, "fit for a king."

So let me tell you exactly, in Elvis's own words, about his home, and why he would never change it.

It is impossible to tell about Graceland without telling about Gladys Presley. The first time Elvis and I met, he was anxious that I meet his "mama." "You'll love her," he said with boyish delight, "everyone does." I'd already had a brief glimpse of Elvis's mother—a beautiful woman with the large, soft brown eyes, pretty dark brown hair, worn simply in natural waves back from her lovely face, and her handsome, tall husband, Vernon Presley—on the set at Paramount studios. But this had been at a considerable distance. Even so, I had noticed the shading of natural darkness around her eyes, the soulful shadows which are so often seen around the eyes of deeply religious, spiritual people. Elvis was exuberant and excited whenever he spoke of her and his love for her.

He went looking for her and his daddy. "They were in a scene for my movie today . . . just sitting in the audience with the extras," he said a bit gleefully. "Mama was a little upset. 'I didn't know, Elvis, or I'd've gone to the beauty parlor and had my hair done,' she said. I told her: 'Mama, you look like an angel just as you are.'" After being unable to locate them, Elvis went looking in another direction, but it turned out they had already returned to the Hollywood Knickerbocker Hotel, where Elvis had taken the entire eleventh floor for his entourage.

Disappointment briefly crossed his face as he returned to say, "They've already gone back to the hotel to pack to go back home. They leave early in the morning. I'm worried about Mama," he confided. "She tires so easily. It's all due to all of her work getting Graceland in shape.

"You'll never know how many hours, actually hundreds, that Mama and I have spent together, planning each room, the décor, colors, carpeting, drapes, furnishings. Even though we've moved in, she's been at it for six months or more. And it's wearing her out. I keep telling her: 'Mama, it doesn't have to be done right now. Take your time. We're in, aren't we? We don't have to have every room finished.' But she's determined to have it perfected before I leave for my army hitch."

What is Graceland like? I remember wondering.

Then Elvis said, a little proudly, for he was happy to have a chance to talk about their new home. "It was a church originally, that sets up on a big sweep of a hill. It is our dream home, Mama's and mine. We had bought a house in a neighborhood that thought we were a nuisance. The neighbors actually asked us to sell our house and move. They couldn't get used to cars driving by and stopping to see where 'that Elvis lived,'" he joked. "It was our first decent house. Mama was so upset. I said, 'Mama, if you want me to, we'll buy up all the neighborhood and they can move.' Mama never wants to inconvenience anyone. She's very timid actually with strangers. Instead, my mama went house looking. And she found this church, a big, empty church building, called 'Graceland.' She fell in love with it—with its big, white columns and all the ground around it. Living here, we would never bother anyone. It meant freedom.'

"'Elvis,' she announced to me, when I got back from a tour, 'I have found the perfect house for us. First, it has a great big attic where we can store all of the things you keep bringing back from your tours. . . .' I laughed because we had our house full of them and no place to put them. Fans were giving me all kinds of things from teddy bears to guitars to baseball bats. You name it. I sure do appreciate the gifts, but they had outgrown our house. And Mama said this big house with this big attic, well we could never outgrow it. She insisted we go and see it right away. I saw the house with Mama. We explored it and it had such possibilities, with some fixing.

"It wasn't a little fixing. It became a year's job.

"You've got to come and see Graceland," Elvis concluded. "See it for yourself. Mama will love having you. Anytime you can come, just let my daddy know and he'll send you a plane ticket and meet you at the airport, like he does our important friends."

"I'd love to Elvis," I replied, "but I have a new home of my own here that I can't very well leave. And my work right now is so pressing, I don't think I can take the time off, not right now."

"I'm sorry, real sorry," he said. Then: "Well someday you've got to see Graceland; let me show it to you. Let me know when." Then: "Now if I go into the army first, and that could happen any day as my service hitch is coming right up. In fact, it was delayed while I finished this picture, *King Creole*. So, if I have to go for those two years first, you can still see Graceland, even if I'm not there. Or there may be furloughs when I can be home. I'll tell my mama and my daddy and they'll be happy to have you."

So much happened right after that. Elvis's mother died suddenly of a hereditary, degenerative liver disease. Elvis told me she was forty-two. He also told me she was five years older than his daddy, and that "a woman being a little older doesn't make any difference in real love because my daddy and my mama are so in love and completely devoted." When I wrote of his mother's death, I put down her age as forty-two, and this information was widely copied. However, her tombstone revealed that she was actually forty-six. But then what woman actually tells her real age?

Heartbreak time came to me also just then. My mother died a few days after Elvis's. Two years later Elvis returned from the service and arrived back in Hollywood to start another picture. That first day we met to take up where we had left off. It was almost a tearful time as we both talked about the unexpected loss of our beloved mothers. He was an only child. I was an only child. And we both lost our mothers at the same time. We shared all this, and it brought us even closer together as friends.

"My mama was so brave and so sick," he said, now sadly remembering back. "She never complained. She kept it to herself . . . so she wouldn't worry us. She came down to Fort Hood, in Texas, and we rented a three-bedroom house, so she and my daddy and I could be together after army hours, on weekends. She cooked. She invited my friends. We had wonderful evenings around the piano, singing gospel. Mama had a beautiful voice. So had my daddy, and with my high baritone . . . we harmonized very well. I always played piano. Yes," Elvis said, "I was never around a piano until a few years ago. I play by ear and practice. We'd spend our time singing, just as we had always done.

"I noticed those dark circles deepening around her beautiful, dear eyes. 'Mama,' I'd say, and hold her and hug her, 'are you all right?' 'Don't worry about me son,' she'd say, and smile—oh so bravely. So very brave. She had so much courage. She must have known how she hurt inside, but she didn't want us to know. I never knew. Then one day she asked Daddy to rush her back to Memphis to her doctor. Seems she was taking a special prescription all of the time. But she never told me. I put them on the train to Memphis and Mama smiled and kissed and hugged me and said, 'Don't worry son, I'll be all right. We'll be together soon.'

"She was rushed into the hospital immediately. And I had word to fly home in a hurry. I got there and she seemed to get better. 'You didn't fly?' she asked. 'You know you shouldn't fly, son,' she said, recalling that time when a plane I was in had dropped down and skidded to such a stop—everyone in it declared, after their scare enabled them to catch their breath, they'd never fly again. And Mama, after I'd told her, made me promise I'd never fly again. I had kept that promise until now. I didn't answer; I just drew her up in my arms and held her, kissing her and loving her and trying to keep my tears from falling on her . . . so she wouldn't know how scared I was now . . . of losing her. For the doctors said it just may be she'd get well. I sat with her all day, telling her about the hundreds of flowers from our fans and so many of them standing outside the hospital praying. She'd get well faster with everyone praying, I told her. She smiled.

"She held on to my hand, and I wanted to give her all of my strength to keep her . . . but she slipped away. She tried so hard to stay for me. But God took her."

Tears streamed down Elvis's cheeks as he talked.

"I know how much you miss her, Elvis."

He said, "I never go up that road to Graceland and to the front door that I don't see my mama coming to the door to greet me—and to run into my arms. She is always there. I see her in every room, every nook and cranny of Graceland. I'll never change any of it. It was all her handiwork, everything. It is all her. Graceland is where I find peace. It will always be my home, because it was my mama's home.

"I dream about her often at night when I'm home," he confided. "Beautiful dreams. Mama is always smiling. I reach out for her and the dream goes. More often I am not so sure it is a dream. I think she is actually there. Sometimes I know she is there . . . even if only so briefly. But she is there. It is a great comfort to me. This only happens . . . at Graceland.

"I never told anyone else about these dreams. They wouldn't understand. But I know you do." For long moments we both sat there quietly with our thoughts, our losses, with our hearts freely exposed to each other's sadness in this time of need for interexchange between the two friends we had become.

Finally, to lighten the moment, I said, "Elvis, please tell me about Graceland. You are always talking about it. Please describe it to me."

"You've got to come and see it," he repeated.

"Let me see it through your eyes, Elvis."

"It sits on a hill above open fields on about eleven acres. All that was there when my mama decided she wanted it were cows." He smiled. "It has twenty-three rooms, and several baths. I keep it all exactly as Mama had it, for it is my mama's house."

Vernon had recently taken a second wife, but it didn't seem polite to inquire about her. Suddenly, though, as if he'd read my mind, Elvis volunteered the following: "Whatever makes my daddy happy is all right with me. I have locked my mother's room. . . . no one's going to live in her room. Besides, there's a whole other wing of the house for them."

Elvis remained thoughtful for a while before continuing. "Mama heard about me being called 'the Rock King' and she decorated my room accordingly. I have an oversize king's bed which sits on a raised dais. One wall is solid mirror and a door in another opens to a whole room that has been made into a walk-in closet. The carpet's red and the furniture is black and white with leather. I have a gold telephone.

"Oh yes"—he smiled—"we have blue ceilings downstairs, and at night, little lights twinkle like stars in a real sky. The kitchen is very modern. We have a big dining-room table with red satin upholstered chairs. It has a beautiful, big crystal chandelier. We can seat twenty-four for dinner. And we do on Thanksgiving and Christmas. Those are our biggest holidays. I'd never be anywhere except home for them.

"Mama and I used to spend so much time buying presents for everyone. Now I do it alone. The living room has a big white piano with gold trim. I had the basement filled in and made into two big rooms for my trophies. The walls are of paneled wood. We have a pool table and slot machines and Coke and candy-bar machines, except you don't have to put money in them. It's all on the house." He grinned.

"Then there's garages, barns, an office, and hen houses for mama's chickens. And a big vegetable garden. And most special of all is mama's rose garden. She loves . . . loved roses. I always promised mama someday I'd give her a big house with lots of bathrooms and a rose garden. I promised her that and we'd look at home picture books together planning that house—when we lived in a place with a hot plate to cook on and shared a bathroom with everyone else who lived there. It was our dreams that kept us going when times were so hard and we were so poor. Dreams are wonderful. I used to ask God how we'd make them come true. I didn't know, but I had faith and so did my mama, that someday . . ." He broke off here, as if talking brought memories that were too painful to say.

"I'll never change the décor that took my mama so many hours and days of her time to make Graceland the kind of a house we loved."

"Never" was a big word that Elvis, at that time, couldn't foresee would change to "hardly ever." At various times over the years of our friendship I'd ask

Elvis about Graceland. He'd say, "It's still the same white outside, with two big, white stone lions on each side of the front door. It's southern colonial style with big white columns. Only things I ever change at all are when drapes or carpets wear out and have to be replaced. It is still mama's house, the way she had it."

Graceland stands on a knoll on Elvis Presley Boulevard. Across the street are honky-tonk-carnival types of hot dog stands and some curio stores. It is not located in an elegant neighborhood, but the house itself and the outlying property enclosed behind a ten-foot-high wall are extremely elegant, especially at night, when blue lights illuminate the house and the driveway, the manicured lawns, pretty flower beds, and magnificent trees.

Elvis was to find that the various women who came into his life would alter his mama's décor. Dee, his father's second wife, and her sons lived there for a time. Elvis told her one day: "I'll build you any kind of house you want, so you can move into your own house. Just draw up the plans." She did so, and a few months later Dee, Vernon, and her three sons moved into their own new house on Dolan Street, with a back gate connecting to the Elvis estate.

The Music Gate, with an image of Elvis and his guitar emblazoned in iron on its front, soon became a tourist's rendezvous and Elvis's uncle Vester Presley and his cousin Harold Lloyd were installed as guards. A room for Elvis's trophies paneled in beautiful white pine, was built onto a wing of the manor. The swimming pool soon had a meditation garden with a fountain and flower beds. "I'm always adding onto it. Mama's home is my hobby," Elvis said.

When Elvis got married, Priscilla was given the privilege of expressing her own decorating impulses.

When she left Elvis, many of the furnishings she had chosen were stored in the attic.

Little Lisa Marie's bedroom, next to Elvis's suite and separated by a dressing room and bath, is decorated in pale yellow and shades of white. Her bed sits on a raised platform with steps. There are shelves for her stuffed toys along the walls. Her bath matches the colors of the room. She has her own tape recorder, stereo, and color-television set.

Elvis's suite boasted a nine-foot-square canopied bed, with two large color-television sets in the ceiling above the bed. Elvis explained this curious fact to me when we were talking about Graceland in Las Vegas. "With two sets, I can watch two programs at the same time." He went on to say that he had added a video-cassette-recording system, stereo music, and a closed-circuit TV monitor. "I can lie in bed"—he laughed—"and see what's going on all over the house. I enjoy watching the fans at the Music Gate. In fact," he said seriously, "the only time I can be private and think and be myself is when I go in my room and shut the door. I like to read and be quiet. Other times, I like to watch TV. Other times, I like to plan my music and my tours . . . so I know exactly what I'm going to do when I come out of that door.

"The only one who can come bursting in is Lisa Marie when she's home with me. Some of our happiest times are spent there, lying on the bed, watching the closed-circuit TV monitor and some regular TV. Lisa Marie has her favorites and there we are, each watching our respective shows. Many times she falls asleep and I pick her up and take her to her own room and put her in her own bed. Next morning at breakfast, she'll ask, 'Daddy, what time was it when I went to sleep?'

"Sometimes we record her singing my songs. She

has real talent, better than me." Elvis laughed. "I keep telling her—even though she sings all of my best songs—she's got to go to school and get the education, like college, that I wish I had. Then, if she wants to be my competition . . . ! Can't you just see us, 'Lisa Marie and Elvis' . . . she's sure to get top billing. But that's at least ten or fifteen years in the future. By then, she'll want her own billing and I'll be at the box office paying to get in to hear her!"

Elvis's living room was huge, with red, overstuffed furniture and scarlet-red plush drapes caught with gold tassles. By 1977 decorative African art objects and a nude glass Venus turning in a waterfall were featured. Many of the paintings were lovely landscapes. The music room adjoining held the large white piano trimmed with gold, while a new trophy room had been added with Elvis's gold records and trophies well displayed.

It was much like his movie sets, furnished dramatically yet in a livable and homelike way at the same time. Some of the rooms might have been in *House Beautiful*.

Sophisticated visitors sometimes questioned Elvis's taste. They have heard so often about some poor untutored entertainer who suddenly hits stardom immediately surrounding himself with art treasures, and they expected Elvis to be like that. It is again to be remembered, as I said earlier, that Elvis, due to the cloistered life he was forced to live, never had the pleasure of visiting art galleries and museums where he could have developed a desire for art collectors' loot. Besides, he was happy just being himself, and this was so typical of Elvis in everything he did: no phony, put-on airs for him. Retaining his simplicity was part of his greatness, and it was one of the many qualities that endeared him to millions and made him a world idol. Good solid decorative pieces that could be purchased at any good furniture store always sufficed. Elvis never tried to "lord it over his fans." Small wonder they could relate to the King. Elvis was precious to us because he stayed one of us.

Graceland underwent another overhaul in decorating when Linda Thompson moved in as Elvis's live-in girl friend, a position she held for four years. Whereas Priscilla had been modest in the changes she made, Linda was more flamboyant and redecorated to suit her tastes.

Elvis said: "No one can go up to the attic—where I keep my mama's sewing machine, the Christmas tree that went round and round playing Christmas carols, and her personal things—and clean house. They are there to stay! I often go up there and sit and visit with them. I can see Mama's reaction at everything up there as I surprised her with them. She was so appreciative, so happy to have them. It never occurred to me to buy her diamond rings and expensive jewelry. I was too young, I guess, to know, and she never asked.

"I thought when I bought Mama a hundred-piece set of silverware one Christmas that was real special. She loved it. And a carving set with pearl handles. She was so proud. But"—he sighed—"I wish I had known about mink and sable coats when I was twenty-two and twenty-three. I'd sure have given them to her.

"I will always keep her car—the first Cadillac, that pink one I bought her—with the first money I made. I keep it polished and running. She was so proud of it. I'll never give it up. I drive it occasionally to keep it ready to go anytime. Mama was so proud of that car . . . even though she didn't drive. My daddy and I drove her, or one of the men working for us. It was her car."

Elvis's estate, according to the inventory filed in probate court, listed Graceland, a Convair 880 Jetliner, a Lockheed Star Nine passenger, a Cadillac, two Stutz Blackhawks, a Ferrari, a Jeep, a Bronco, a Chevy pickup, a Scout, and three tractors, seven motorcycles, three mobile houses, seven golf carts, six horses, and Lisa Marie's Shetland pony cart.

Among the numerous pieces of jewelry listed were Elvis's famous Maltese cross, studded with 236 diamonds, and a great number of rings. His trophy room, holding his famous gold records and sixteen cabinets with locks for his many citations, including many karate honors he had won, recording equipment, eighteen television sets—all these were listed among various household effects.

Elvis's wardrobe at the time of his death consisted of thirty custom-made, elegant suits, besides costumes valued at many thousands of dollars, one hundred pairs of trousers, jeweled vests, a hundred pairs of shoes and boots, shirts, handkerchiefs, scarves, ties, underwear, and many other items too numerous to mention.

Elvis, a very giving person, frequently cleaned out his wardrobe closets. One day, when he was living in his Monovale Drive house in Holmby Hills adjacent to Beverly Hills, California, he walked into the kitchen with his arms loaded with his clothes. Four trips from his wardrobe closet that morning resulted in the huge kitchen table being piled with everything from jeans and sweaters to white-fox-trimmed capes. "Help yourself, everybody," he announced to the Memphis Mafia boys and whoever else was there.

"Anything you can't use, give it to someone, anyone who can."

To my surprise I had a telephone call from a girl who said her boyfriend had fallen heir to some of Elvis's apparel at this "give-away-Elvis's-clothes day." "We have a black-fox-trimmed velvet suit, three satin, custom-made shirts with inside labels embroidered 'custom made for Elvis.' Would you know some Elvis fans who would like to buy them?"

"How much?"

"The shirts cost Elvis $150 a piece," she said. "And the black fox and velvet suit $1500. We'll take $500 for it."

Later on I saw silk shirts in a window in Hollywood, exactly as she had described them, with a sign, "Custom made for and worn by Elvis, $100 each."

On the disclosure of the contents of Elvis's estate, offers poured in from all directions, mostly from salespeople who were anxious to obtain Elvis's personal belongings. They would bring them a fortune from Elvis fans, many of whom had paid as much as $100 for just a piece of a sheet Elvis had reportedly slept on at a hotel.

Of the hundreds of portraits fans painted and sent to Elvis, only one large portrait of Elvis hung at Graceland. None had been known to be painted by an artist of national reputation. This is not surprising. Jayne Mansfield's pink palace held many portraits of her painted by fans, but not one painting was done by a well-known artist. She never thought to commission such a work, perhaps no more than Elvis did, living as she did such a busy life of always being photographed and standing before cameras.

Elvis always said: "Graceland will always be my home—forever." Did Elvis know that he would be buried there in the Meditation Garden? Perhaps he did, since one of his natural-born gifts was ESP. He amazed those of us close to him by his ability to see the past, present, and the future—and all so accurately! Few people knew of this special gift and Elvis, in this as in everything else, was too modest to consider ever exploiting it or even talking about it publicly.

20. "My Visit with Elvis at Graceland"
by Bob Wayne

Elvis and Graceland:
The Mythical Legend and the Facts

Unmasking the Mystery of Graceland and Elvis

NOTE: We've heard what the Elvis detractors had to say about Graceland—and most of them were lucky if they even saw it. Now let's hear the real truth from a lucky fan who had the great good fortune not only to see Elvis's beautiful mansion but to meet with Elvis in person.—M.M.

You hear about people collecting for hours, outside the gates of Elvis Presley's famous home Graceland on Highway 51 outside of Memphis. They pick up stones from the gravel on the side of the road—for souvenirs.

Graceland, as the world knows, has become a legendary myth—a fortress, armored with shotguns and guards! To me, who went to school with Elvis at Hume, it didn't add up. The Presleys weren't that kind of people at all. They were nice humble down-to-earth folks. But then, money and fame can change the best!

I had been long gone these past several years of Elvis's increasing fame. I'd had no reason to contact him or the Presleys. But during the recent holidays I decided to go home and see my grandparents. And one morning I had the urge and I shoved off and went over to see Elvis.

Call? No. Southern people don't pay visits that way. You just show up and there's always a welcoming hand.

At a service station I asked the gas pumper to level with me. Was Elvis high hat nowadays? Was he turning down old friends? The guy said "nope," but that to get into Graceland, the best thing to do was to go down the road a piece and stop by Elvis's father's new home first. Vernon is just the same guy as he always was—and he would no doubt tell me how to crash Graceland.

"I didn't want to crash," I explained.

The pump guy said, "Why not? I hear everybody else tries!"

I went down to Vernon's home, and his wife answered the door. They have a modern pretty home with, say, four bedrooms. They were just having their coffee and they asked me in.

I said, "I hear Graceland is a real fortress these days."

Vernon laughed. "Who told you that?" he said. Then realizing that I'd been away a long time he said, "If you'd like to go over, we'll take a stroll."

"Elvis usually sleeps until about one or two. He's a
night owl, listens to music all night and sleeps in late.
We won't disturb him—unless he's up. But come
along!"

Mrs. Presley, Vernon's second wife, said her sons
had never really had a good look at all of Elvis's trophies, and it being a Saturday, and them being home
from school, she said to them, "Come along. We'll go
too!" They seemed to be quite polite, well-mannered
kids. Mrs. Presley seemed a terribly nice woman.

We went out the back door and down a garden
path in back that led to a big fence. There was a
place in the fence pretty worn from climbing over
and pushing it down. And we went through it. There
we were right on the grounds of the famous legendary Graceland.

The fences were painted white. Everything was in
apple-pie order. "Elvis dotes on this place, wants it
shipshape and perfect like a well-greased car in operation," Vernon remarked. You could see that.

Being there in the back of Graceland's acres in like
being on a big farm. You see chicken houses, geese
houses, pigeon coops. And all kinds of farmyard fowl
were clucking. Everything was meticulously neat and
painted. And there was plenty of green lawn.

Elvis has four dogs. Each one has a house. There
are other animals too, some very rare. His cats usually
stay in the house with Elvis. And I learned that his
monkey "Scatter," which Elvis got several years ago,
had died.

Dead center in the back are the garages with Elvis's
cars. There's the Rolls, in fact two of them, and a
sports car. And there's two elaborate golf carts. In another there's Elvis's motorcycles and his mother's pink
Cadillac. The latter is polished and in top condition

even though it is a 1957. Elvis says he'll never part with it, for it was his mother's pride and joy.

Then there's Elvis's business offices with his staff of secretaries who take care of his enormous fan mail. We dropped by to meet the girls, all of whom looked like beauty-contest winners. Vernon assured me that they are all highly competent, as Elvis is a perfectionist. While he likes attractive people around him, they have to cut the mustard too.

In his office-cottage there is a room that looks like a library with neatly bound leather volumes of Elvis's favorite press clippings. So don't let anyone tell you he never reads what is written about him. There were sacks and sacks of fan mail. The secretaries told me they read it all and sort out the more important ones and the ones they feel would be interesting for Elvis to read. Naturally he can't read them all.

Leaving the office-cottage, we walked up the path to the back door of Graceland. Elvis's mother got her family trained to use the back door, "to save much wear and tear on her carpets coming into the front," Vernon said and laughed. "And we still have that habit of coming in the back door."

Inside we found Elvis's grandmama who is his housekeeper. She was peeling potatoes and a maid was busying herself rolling out piecrust.

"It is always open house for Elvis's friends," Vernon explained. "You never know if there will be Elvis for dinner—or a dozen. You never know. He believes in true southern hospitality."

Elvis's Memphis Mafia, as they are called, don't live at Graceland. They all have their own homes. Many of the boys are married and have their own families. They only live with Elvis when he is in Hollywood making movies.

"Elvis is still asleep," his grandmama said, "so be

quiet! He has that habit of turning day into night
and night into day." She smiled, but not in a reprov-
ing manner.

We tiptoed through the big rooms to the front en-
trance. When we opened the door, I was shocked!
There were all kinds of people milling about out
front. They were not on the highway peering up at
the Graceland forest. They were on the inside, right
there at the door. And they were all behaving very or-
derly and quiet.

"How come? Do you let the public walk right into
Graceland?" I asked Vernon in astonishment. "I've always heard no one could get in past the guards at the
gate!"

Vernon laughed indulgently. "Don't believe all that
paper talk," he said easily. "We have gatekeepers, and
when Elvis is at home and he wants privacy, the big
iron gates are kept locked. The gatekeepers, as you
can see, are friendly polite people, interested in Elvis's fans. They will talk to them and tell them all
about Graceland and answer all of their questions,
much like guides do when you visit a museum."

That is what Graceland will someday become. Already Elvis has rooms and rooms filled with trophies
and mementos, each marking a stride forward in his
career.

Elvis has been asked by various institutes to contri-
bute all of this for an Elvis Presley Room for a
museum. But he has said, when he is through with
his home, someday, maybe he'll open it as a museum
here, in memory of his mother who loved the place so
much.

I was stunned. It was all so different than what I
had always read about. "When did this happen, that
you began letting the public come in and take over
the grounds of Graceland?" I asked.

"Elvis will tell you about it," Vernon said. By this time Vernon and Mrs. Presley were engulfed by fans with their cameras. The two stood there pleasantly posing for pictures which were being snapped by the hundreds. You could hear voices piping up, "That's Elvis's dad and his stepmom." Everything was as pleasant as a tea party on the lawns of Buckingham Palace in England.

Suddenly the gatekeeper gave a small whistle . . . Vernon turned. It was a signal that said Elvis was awake and up! And it was time to close the gates, to get the crowds out. Otherwise Elvis couldn't come outside, or he'd be kept there for hours visiting with the people. And Elvis, too, has things to do.

At times Elvis will give the signal and call the gatekeeper to let the people stay on, and if he's free and so inclined, he'll come out and talk to everyone and pose for pictures, his father said. "But today he has a busy day, I guess."

The people left and the big gates clanged shut. And it was again the fortress, the remote Graceland that I had always read about.

Vernon and I walked back up to the front of the house, and we went inside. Elvis came bounding down the stairs—with a smile. He was in great spirits. He gave his daddy a big hug and a kiss on the cheek. He was affectionate. He bounced into the kitchen to give his grandmama a big hug and kiss, and to ask, "*What* are we having for dinner?"

"Land, you haven't had breakfast yet Elvis!" she chided. "Dinner isn't until supper time!"

"I'm starved," Elvis announced.

He sat down for bacon and eggs, which were served up to him immediately. After he had finished, he took me through the house. He has so many trophies that he could right this minute fill a museum!

"How come Elvis," I asked, "you let the public come into your grounds? The whole world thinks getting into Graceland is like crashing the Bank of England!"

"Well, it came about naturally," Elvis replied. "Mama used to go down to the gate, when she was alive, every afternoon, and visit with everyone outside. Then, as you can see, this highway got so built-up with all of that business on the other side that it became a real traffic problem, with cars slowing up to take a look! Then it got so the traffic got snarled with cars stopping and this area out front became a road hazard. It was actually unsafe for drivers.

"I said to my daddy, why not let the people come in and walk around and enjoy the grounds—as often as we can. So we do."

"Did this just happen? Because no one knows about it," I said.

"No, it's been going on for the last three years." Elvis laughed. "People can drive in and park and walk about as they wish. Just like a public park." He smiled. "At times, if I've been working hard, we keep it closed. But usually the gates are open every afternoon from two to five."

Outside there were still people clinging to the gates. "Come on out, Elvis, we want your picture?" some of them called. Elvis walked down and obliged. I tagged along!

"Everything is so different than what I have been reading about you," I said.

"We don't notice much what they write about Graceland." He laughed again. "Of course, we haven't got a big sign up that says 'Welcome, enter,' or it might get out of hand! As long as it doesn't people are welcome to share it with me. It's these people that made it possible for me to have it in the first place!"

We walked back up the path to the big front door. "Stay for supper," Elvis invited. "Grandmama cooks a real southern ham and black-eyed peas. That's what's on for tonight!"

To Elvis "dinner" was still "supper."

"You'll have to excuse me," he said. "I've got some appointments. Let Grandmama know if you'll be staying. You staying to eat, Daddy?" he called back to Vernon.

Elvis was off through the house and out the back door. In split seconds you could hear the roar of his motorcycle and the big gates opening. Elvis was roaring down the highway—happy with his world.

"Is anyone afraid Elvis will be kidnapped with all of this open access to his home and grounds?" I asked.

His grandmama's eyes twinkled. "Everyone loves Elvis," she said simply. "No one would ever try that."

"Say, what about Priscilla Beaulieu," I asked. "Are she and Elvis secretly married?"

"Goodness, no. She's a real sweet girl," his grandmama replied.

It's almost impossible to believe—unless you know the southern people, their trust, and their faith in humanity. What other star would open his home to the public like Elvis?

21. Aboard Elvis's Luxury Jet, the <u>Lisa Marie</u>

The sky was overhung with soft gray clouds that only permitted an intermittent glimpse of the sun. In spite of the cold, hundreds of fans and sightseers hung around the Music Gate at Graceland. All were hoping that Elvis would come out. He was in town. He was in residence, and it would be only a ten-to-one—no, a hundred-to-one shot that he just might drive out the Music Gate. Often he detoured to a back-road gate to avoid the crowds. When he was feeling well, he would come to the Music Gate. But as Uncle Vesper Presley would tell you, "Elvis hasn't been feeling well for a long time. And he seldom comes to the gate even though he might have wanted to."

Elvis was always appreciative of his fans and gracious to them. He had welcomed them often. He gave orders to open the gate when he was not at home, so his fans could come in and see the grounds and look around. What other superstar in the history of the entertainment world had ever allowed that? Elvis appreciated his fans. He often told them so many, many times on concert tours. He would say, "I wouldn't have all of this—if it were not for you!"

One handsome young couple had waited since early dawn by the Music Gate. They had driven from California—with the one express purpose and determination of seeing or at least glimpsing and hopefully meeting Elvis in person. The man and his wife had taken turns going across the street to buy snacks during their long day's wait so that one was always in front of the gate.

"It was now midnight. A light rain had started to fall," recalled the husband, who was possibly near Elvis's age. "My wife and I were huddled in our car to keep warm, when suddenly the gate opened and out came Elvis on his three-wheeler. Like greased lightning, he headed down Elvis Presley Boulevard . . . with us in hot pursuit. This was the golden opportunity we had waited for. Speed was no objective. If we got a ticket and were stopped, we might lose Elvis. We gave our all going after him. Suddenly from a hidden road, another car popped out to also join us in hot pursuit of Elvis. Elvis came to a halt at the Memphis airport, where he went inside. He turned to take a look at us, for he had seen us following him through his rear-vision mirror.

"To our delight he spoke and said, 'You've been following me?' We nodded assent. In the friendliest manner, he reached out his hand and said, 'I'm Elvis Presley. How are you?' You can't imagine our reaction of pure pleasure in shaking his hand. My wife was very excited, and so was I. But we tried to act normal and civil.

" 'It is going to rain harder,' Elvis said. 'Would you

like to come aboard my plane, the *Lisa Marie*, parked
out there?'

"Would we? It was like an invitation to heaven, for
we were indeed long dedicated in our admiration of
Elvis and his work. Now, here he was, acting just like
one of us. No airs. No pretense, just natural and
gracious and as my wife said, so charming, without
trying to be."

I should mention here that Elvis was especially
pleased and proud of the *Lisa Marie*, the jet on
which he most preferred to travel during the last
three years of his life. The *Lisa Marie* was a Convair
880 which was converted under Elvis's personal super-
vision into the most luxurious flying penthouse ever
known. He paid a half-million dollars for the plane,
which was designed to carry eighty-three passengers.

First Elvis had the interior completely stripped.
Being very artistic himself, Elvis then proceeded to
completely redesign the interior and have it refitted
with a luxurious lounge. For this lounge he ordered a
pair of magnificently plush couches—one bronze-
colored, one apple-green—each costing $22,000—and a
gaming table with equally plush, tufted chairs, as well
as a bar, two television sets, and two vending
machines stocked to the brim with candy bars. For his
bedroom Elvis ordered a nine-foot-square bed and
pale blue silk sheets with a stunning blue bedspread
and matching furnishings. The bed alone cost $14,-
000. The bathroom had a pure gold washbasin and
gold faucets with a wall-size lighted mirror. In addi-
tion to the lounge and bedroom, Elvis's private jet
contained a conference room, decorated in green and
beige; the swivel chairs in this room, flamboyantly
upholstered in a rosy-white shade of leather that
could only be called flamingo, cost $7,000 each. A mi-
crowave oven in the plane's galley was capable of

producing twenty-three complete gourmet dinners within a few minutes, and its massive refrigeration equipment could stock a month's supply of meats, vegetables, and fruit fit for—what else?—a king.

Altogether, the plane contained four TV sets, an elaborate stereo system that piped music into no less than fifty-two speakers that were carefully placed throughout its enormous length. The communications system, which included seven sky telephones, enabled Elvis to dial anywhere and speak with anyone in the world. The intercom in his bedroom enabled him to talk with anyone on the plane any time he so wished. The call signs of the *Lisa Marie*, which, of course, was named after his daughter, were "Hound Dog 1" and "Hound Dog 2." Even though there was a bar, there was no alcohol aboard.

Elvis once told me that the *Lisa Marie* was well equipped for overseas flying and that all in all he thought it was just fantastic. He said that he wound up spending a total of a million and a half dollars in realizing his plans for the *Lisa Marie*—all of it in cash. "We never try to spend money that we don't have. Flying in this plane is quite a switch from when I started out in the business, driving an old 1954 black Cadillac. At that time, I thought I had reached pure luxury with such a car, even though it was secondhand."

Elvis's favorite colors, blue and white, were used on the exterior of the *Lisa Marie* as well as his two other planes. The tails of his planes all bore the gold letters "TCB" (Taking Care of Business). Elvis had only to lift his telephone to summon his own personal flying crew and say, "We fly in an hour." And an hour later, no more, no less, the *Lisa Marie* was speeding down the runway, ready for flight.

It was on this magical jet that the lucky husband

and wife, who had waited so patiently in the rain for just a glimpse of their idol, suddenly found themselves. They could hardly believe their good fortune. But this was only the beginning, for once they had boarded the *Lisa Marie*, Elvis graciously and modestly invited them on a tour of its plush interior. According to the husband, "It's living room, bedrooms, kitchen—just everything was beautiful and in perfect order.

" 'There's too much rain to take off tonight,' Elvis said, 'so we might as well sit down and talk.' He ordered coffee, sandwiches, and cake, and we sat there, the five of us. He had also invited the other two who had joined in the mad chase to catch up with him. We were sitting there enjoying his company, for he put us perfectly at ease. Outside the rain came down harder. Elvis said many times he slept on his plane when the weather was too bad to take off. The crew were aboard and ready for flight, so Elvis told them to take off and get home with their families. They'd have to wait until the weather cleared, perhaps the next day.

"There was soft music playing, emanating from hidden speakers throughout the plane. Then came singing—some of Elvis's own hits. Thoughtlessly, in our excitement I asked, 'Who is that singing on those records, Elvis?'

"He laughed, shrugged his shoulders. 'Well, some singer, but I don't think he'll get very far, do you?' Of course Elvis was the singer. He grinned. He had a marvelous, dry sense of humor.

"We asked him when he would be going back to Hollywood to make more movies.

"Elvis replied, 'First I want to get a good script. I want to make another two or three pictures, just to show I can act. My dream is pretty far out I know, but I'd like to win an Oscar. . . . I guess all actors wish for that esteem. . . . No, not necessarily esteem—but to have your peers say you are good at your work. That's it. I hope to get in shape as soon as I get my health A-1 again, then I'll make a picture.

" 'I want to have my own producing company. And have my own say. All of those movies I made—I never had any approval of any part of them. I was just handed a script and told, "Go to it, Elvis, this is it!" The Colonel arranged all of that. A million dollars a movie, the music rights, and 50 percent of the take . . . which was a pretty hefty take, I well know. I never backed off. There came the time I got tired of standing in front of that box, the cameras, and doing the same old thing over and over. I wanted a role that would be challenging, something I could deal with, feel inside of me. It got to the point,' Elvis said, 'that I had had it. . . . I had to get out before live audiences again. I had to come alive again. The formula movies were getting stale and boring to me as well'—he laughed—'as I guess to a lot of other people. The Colonel said they always made money, in fact a lot of money.' Elvis paused reflectively. 'And that was the issue, money. I wanted more than money—much more—to feel and know I was doing something worthwhile. A constant formula routine sameness in anything is not fulfilling or rewarding, no matter the money take.'

"Elvis began talking about Hollywood. 'It's Tinseltown—no real values out there,' he said. 'I would never want to make it my home. No way, man, no way.'

"My wife asked Elvis if it wasn't exciting dating all of the gorgeous film stars like Ann-Margret, Juliet Prowse—to name a couple we had read he had dated. Elvis smiled. 'They are very nice women, but they are actresses. Their careers come first over everything else. A career can become a very empty possession, and a very lonely one. Take me, I know.'

"Elvis did not look well. His face was puffy, white, and pale. His body was puffy. He was dressed immaculately although in a casual shirt, pants, and jacket. Nothing fancy.

" 'I'm not putting actresses down,' Elvis explained. 'They are especially beautiful and full of talent. To get way up as high as they are, they have to be dedicated to their careers to do it. It's—well, Hollywood is dog-eat-dog in a business sense. Friendships are usually based on business and what it will get them. It's so different than here, at home in Memphis.

" 'My home will always be Memphis—and my kind of people. We are just ordinary people, nothing fancy . . . but honest and hardworking and believing in God and the Ten Commandments, and living up to them every day. Honesty is a prime requisite to me,' Elvis explained. 'I can't tell you how much I admire and love honest people. Not the phony people who slap you on the back and don't mean all the fancy words they tell you. I love my home, Graceland, and it will always be my home.'

"Elvis, during the course of the wee, small hours, mentioned his mother and how precious she was to him. And his daddy and then his little girl, Lisa Marie. 'She's coming out to spend the summer with me soon as school's out. She's the real joy of my life. She makes my life worth every effort.'

"Elvis suddenly became quiet, like he was talked out. We sat there listening to the rain patter and the music, knowing we should be going. And realizing Elvis was too polite to tell us to go. Finally we were able to pull ourselves away, and say, 'thank you' and 'good-bye.' And Elvis said, 'Good-bye and God bless you.'

"It was one of the most memorable and incredible nights of our lives. Always it will be the highlight of our lives!"

This account of a personal meeting with Elvis was given to me by this young couple who waited an hour to get my undivided time and attention when I was appearing at Northridge, California, in the Topanga Mall Shopping Center to set the record straight on Elvis.

22. How Elvis Suffered and Died

Elvis knew fully well for the last three years of his life that he was dying. But this information was kept from the public and even from Elvis's family. While they surmised much, and everyone close to Graceland worried about Elvis's continuing sickness and his frequent if brief hospitalizations, no one wanted to say what their eyes told them was true—that Elvis's heart was seriously strained from overwork and that he was slowly but surely succumbing to a growing fatigue. In 1975 Elvis learned he had bone cancer in both legs, which sent him into a deep depression. Hadn't he suffered enough already?

Despite his depression, Elvis kept on going. And Elvis was still going, making all the efforts he could possibly make to put on a brave front, that fateful morning of August 16, 1977. He had visited his dentist at two-thirty A.M. He had driven home to play a few sets of racquet ball. At nine A.M. he had gone into his bathroom. Five hours later he was found, his face blue, barely breathing and in a coma from which he would never awaken.

What had happened?

Wild accounts—and there were many of these—were given. Elvis was in his pajamas, his eyes open, blood-shot and red, and staring vacantly. A bodyguard called his father and the Memphis hospital to rush an ambulance. Elvis's doctor, who was with him at all times, was in another room of the house and rushed in. He started mouth-to-mouth resuscitation en route to the hospital, all the while saying, pleading over and over, "Elvis, breathe for me! Presley, breathe for me!" It was to no avail. Elvis had already passed out of this life.

What had happened to Elvis during those five hours there on the bathroom floor? With a whole house filled with family and friends and servants, why hadn't he called for help? His girl friend, Ginger Alden, was asleep on his bed, only the closed bathroom door between them. Why hadn't he called for help?

"It will be the same thing that took my mother," Elvis had said a short time before these tragic events. "I became quite ill three years ago, and as the times pass, I realize I am destined for an early parting from this life to the next one." Elvis told me this with the quiet assurance of one who was resigned to the inevitable and had made his peace. He observed, "Naturally, I get periods of depression. Some of it is due to all of the doctoring, the secret hospital stays, all the medication to keep me going. I want, the dear Lord knows, to be well and healthy and feel vigorous again.

"The long confinements I've had to endure as a prisoner of my fame have been filled with desperation and frustration. I've longed for freedom to be like other people. I never dare to go out for fear of causing a riot. The whole career thing has gotten so out of hand.

"It all started when the Colonel and the boys used to ignite the commotion by getting a few girls to start yelling, 'There's Elvis!' It kept growing . . . like I'm some kind of freak. It is actually more than any human being can live with . . . not to be able to go out the door . . . walk the street . . . go into stores . . . do things all free people in this country can do . . . except me! But I made the agreement with Colonel Parker: this was to be my image. 'Keep 'em curious, always wanting more.' My word and my honor are 100 percent good. I've been stuck with this straitjacket since 1954! No one knows how boring the long hours and staying inside, confined, get. Sometimes I feel I'll explode."

Now Elvis had died. The doctors said: "Death was due to a massive heart attack. He suffered no pain." Others said it was an overdose of drugs; they said terrible things about Elvis, things which upset all of us who knew him, and knew the truth—that he was only on medications prescribed by his doctor. He was never hooked on heroin, never involved in the mainline-drugs scene in any way whatsoever. No matter how many times the examining doctors, coroner, and pathologists, after the autopsy, firmly said, "Elvis was never on drugs," some gossip reporters persisted in saying he was. I did my best to tell the facts, and the truth. For who else was there?

A month after Elvis's passing, full on indignation for the lies being spoken of Elvis, and full of sorrow for the wrongs being done to Elvis, I spent a good deal of time in meditation, prayer, and in consultation with medical specialists, trying to uncover how exactly Elvis had died. The conclusion I have reached is that Elvis suffered terribly. No one could hear him call out for help because he was helpless to call out loud enough to be heard!

A famous internist and pharmacologist who knew Elvis well gives this report: "Elvis was not on dope. Yes, lots of medicine. But not dope, and not alcohol either. He never in his life drank any form of alcohol. There was a deep fear in him. He had long worried about his health, for he kept getting worse instead of better the last three years, in spite of the medication and his frequent trips to the hospital. He kept exercising in spite of the deep, constantly growing fatigue, he experienced. At times, he was often onstage, and he was not sure of himself due to this overpowering lifelessness inside him, but he was doing his best. He loved performing, and he loved his fans. He exerted himself beyond his strength only to please, and not for the money . . . money which had not brought him happiness. Toward the last, he held money in actual contempt. People around him were so greedy. He was fully aware of their greed and gave so much to them, saying, 'It's only money.' Blinded by their greed, these people were unseeing of Elvis's true feelings, which otherwise would have shamed them for using him so. There were so few, almost none, he could trust.

"Elvis had a brilliant mind, a powerful intellect. Yet he also possessed an almost naive kindness along with an outgoing and helpful nature. He needed love, lots of it—and he responded to everyone with love. He was born religious, and his faith became even stronger as he got older."

Elvis was seated on the toilet, actually reading a religious book, that last morning of his life. He was deeply into religion. He knew the Bible thoroughly,

as well as something about all religions. He had read
much and continued reading up to the end. Here was
Elvis reading, when suddenly a terrible pain gripped
him in his stomach and seized his heart with a stran-
gler's grip. He fell crashing to the floor.

"Oh no, dear dear God," he thought in panic and
terror. "Not now. Not this way. Please, dear God,
dear God, dear God." But no words came from him.
They were all deep inside of him. He was suffering
terrible, excruciating pain. He could not breathe. He
gasped for air, lying there, trying to get up. He
couldn't move. He couldn't get up. He had to get up.
He must get up. He must, so he could breathe. He lay
there completely helpless, gasping for air. Still, he
could not move. With one supreme effort, he tried
with all the desperation he felt, and his knees gave
way and he fell back, completely spent. That terrible
pain, like swords of fire, jabbing, slitting, cutting into
his stomach, and especially his liver—it was impossible
to bear.   "Please, dear God," he begged inwardly,
the sweat pouring from his brow, streaming in agony
down his face and from his entire body. "Help me.
Oh, Good Lord, help me," he pleaded. Tears
streamed down his cheeks. Still he could not move.
He lay there motionless, inwardly screaming—yelling
for help—the words, "Help! Please help me!"—flashing
through him. There were no sounds. His tongue would
not move. No sound came from him.

Elvis suffered terribly. But finally he resigned himself, and, with a very deep sense of depression, accepted that the end had come. Elvis knew this was
the end, and he knew everything that had been happening to him, for he had long expected it, dreaded
it, knowing it would come. But he had not known it
would be now—so soon. Too soon. He had so much to

live for. Even with all of his pain and sickness, he wanted to live.

Now he fully knew death had taken hold of him. There was no need to fight it. And with this complete resignation and acceptance, the pain gradually and slowly released him.

Hopeless, he lay there for at least two more hours, alive and helpless. Occasionally the pain, that horrible raging, tearing pain that had cut his body to ribbons, let up for a moment. "Thank you, Dear Lord, for easing it—this burning, searing of my flesh. It is like being . . . *crucified!* Oh, dear God, dear Lord," he cried inwardly in such anguish. Suddenly the thought flashed through him: this must be like what Jesus suffered.

His mother is the one who stands by him now. He relaxes. The tight muscles on his face and neck soften. "Mama, Mama." He looks at her through those staring eyes which are now the eyes of his spirit. He sees in wonder his earthly chest which is still heaving with earthly pain—unwilling to give up the struggle. "Mama, you are holding my hand." He looks up at her face and the pain is now gone—completely. His body is filled with relief and a sublime, relaxing wonderment that he has never known before. "You are here to take me?" his spirit asks.

She smiles. "Yes, my dear son. My beloved son. I am here all of this time . . . for I knew that now was your time to cross over to the other side, to my side." Taking his hand, she stays with him . . . and watches over him. And he is now confident, content, happy and without fear.

Elvis is still alive, physically, when the bathroom door finally, after all those agonizing five hours, bursts open. And soon people are all around him saying, "Breathe, Presley! Breathe, Presley!" But now at last, he is standing by his mother, and he looks at his mortal body, and the anguish of the people who are desperately trying to revive him.

His father rushes into the room. Elvis wants to say a good-bye to him. But his mother shakes her head. Elvis is now no longer in his mortal state. As he turns to leave with her . . . his little daughter, Lisa Marie, runs in the room, terrified. "What's happened to my daddy?" she cries out. Someone grabs her and walks the child away, so she won't see Elvis's body lying there, now slowly turning blue.

"If I could just tell Lisa Marie good-bye . . ." Elvis is sad . . . his little girl whom he loved so much. He hears the shrieking sirens of an ambulance racing up the drive to Graceland. Lisa Marie is being led out of the room. "If I could have only held her and kissed her, and told her we will be together again someday . . ." Now it is too late. The white, shining light that his mother is leading him into enfolds them, and they are lost to the world.

After Elvis's death, many people reported having had dreams about him.

One of these people wrote to me. "He has slept and rested," she said. "Now he is fully awake and fully aware of what has happened to him . . . his rebirth and the heaven where he now finds himself. There is Elvis, even in a prankish mood, standing, and he smiles. It is like he wants us to know he is happy and well."

A Christian minister reports the following dream of Elvis: "Elvis, without sound, communicates his feelings about his former associates who said so many lies about him. At the time he was deeply hurt, but now he has forgotten all about it. There are so many more important things for him to do."

An Elvis Presley fan club president from England, who writes to me often, has written these words: "I fasted and prayed for months for some sign that Elvis is well. One night a light opened at the end of my room and there was Elvis. I strongly sensed there was an invisible curtain I was looking through, and I could not jump out of bed and reach him. Elvis, I learned, is very concerned about his child, little nine-year-old Lisa Marie. He spoke no vocal words, but his thoughts came through as though spoken, and clearly. He will see to it that no harm is done to her, that she will not be kidnapped. Also, he is anxious that someone talk to little Lisa Marie who can help the child out of the deep depression she is in. She needs a friend she can trust, a doctor or someone else to help her on her side. Elvis cannot do it all by himself. He and his mother are both doing everything they can to help her from their side."

One of Elvis's music men said: "When Elvis sang 'Love Me Tender' on TV, his whole aura was pink. He knew his audience. He was a good actor. When he sang 'Where Do I Go,' he had all white lights around his whole body . . . the highest spiritual light anyone can have. I can believe that Elvis in the spirit world is trying to influence composers to go more into the spiritual way. And I believe he is looking for one who will awaken the people by music and bring them back to God. Elvis long saw his future in this line of work—rather than the Hollywood-side scene."

Shortly after these disclosures, people I'd never known or met continued writing to me daily and calling me and giving me their own personal stories about and experiences with Elvis. Years of research could never, in any degree or way, bring so much exclusive information to light; mere research could never assemble all the people, from all walks of life, who wanted to tell their personal feelings and experiences, to share the truth about the real Elvis Presley, as he really was and is—all the people who shared their truths with me so that I could now share it with all my readers.

Shortly after Elvis's demise, when I was in a state of deepest grief and shock, I was forced to emerge from my heartbreak to answer an urgent phone call from Bobby Morris, Elvis's conductor/arranger, calling from Las Vegas. "Elvis really loved you, May," Bobby said. "He trusted you. God knows you two used to talk about everything under the sun. Elvis often said: 'If I could choose one person to take a long plane trip with me, she would be the one. May is well read, knows everyone, has an intellectual mind, and is great fun to have around. I learn a lot from her.

'I love May Mann,' he used to say. 'She's for real. She always writes the truth as it is. She's asked me every question in the world, even about sex and religion, in the last few weeks, knowing how really sick I am. I've even talked to her about my health, which is pretty well shot, as you well know. And about 'drugs,' and how my false pals try to betray me . . . instead of calling it my medicine, prescribed by my doctor. When I'm gone, I hope she tells it as it is, about what I've said. I've told her that.' "

With his remarkable gift for seeing the future which always amazed me, Elvis had once called, and had uttered these words of true prophecy: "I know from some of the hate mail I've received, from crummy people I've never even met, there's a lot of real sick sick sick people out there. *The hour I die, their hate machines will start going.*" These were Elvis's own true words.

"I've asked God, why? There's some of the boys who work for me . . . the 'Memphis Mafia.' Some of them have already turned, and a couple more I can see will do the same . . . if given the chance.

"I've called you, May, because you're the only one I know I can depend on to speak for me if that time should come. You have known how long I've been so sick. Those last times in Las Vegas, doctors kept pumping me with shots to stave off the pain, to keep me going . . . keep the money machine going. I'd plead I was too sick to go back onstage.

"I want it known as my mama in heaven knows and my daddy knows, I was never a junkie. I never took drugs for kicks . . . nor did I ever, before God, mainline or anything like that. My mind is always clear. I'm never spaced out or stoned. But I knew what the guys around me were doing. I was always aware. And I've been reading the Bible to them for years. They only listen halfway and go on doing as they please. I've had to get some of them out of plenty of scrapes, even jail.

"My daddy has wanted to fire most of them a dozen different times, and sometimes he has. They always come back, crying for forgiveness. The Bible says 'turn the other cheek' . . . and pray they will be better. I have spent half of my career getting them out of trouble. It's like I'm the father of my clan. My daddy has told me again and again I've been too good to them.

"You and I have talked hundreds of times on every subject in the world. During some of those 'one-hundred-question sessions'—there wasn't anything you didn't ask me—I was a little embarrassed when you asked how I felt about sex—kinky sex—adultery, women, even death. It took you all of those eighteen years before you got the courage to ask me about sex—sleeping around, VD, all of it.

"When I'm gone, tell it all just as I said it. I know you will. I was never the complete fool that the boys who worked for me, who shared the good life, for whom I bought expensive cars, clothes, jewelry, homes . . . who had it all just as good as me . . . I was never the complete patsy and fool they took me for. They think I am a religious nut. I have always been close to God, ever since I can remember.

"Way back, when my daddy and my mama and me lived in that little shanty in Tupelo, our only happiness was going to church. And our sing-a-longs, with all our black neighbors sitting on their stoops at night, singing country and the blues. Our harmonizing would go all up and down the dirt roads we lived on . . . sometimes like half a mile. Mama would be rocking in her chair and we'd sway and rock . . . that's when I learned to rock the blues. Man, those were great times.

"I'm one southern boy who's never left the South. It is the dearest place in the world to me. So is Tennessee and all of our kind of folks. Here's where I'm comfortable and happy. I've only been out of the United States twice. Once in Germany in the service, and in Acapulco to make a film.

Those hundred-question interviews with Elvis contain in Elvis's own words, his anticipation of attackers.

"I know the characteristics of my believed-to-be trusted good old southern boys!" he said during one of these interviews. "In the beginning, we were all like brothers. But some along the way have already proven themselves to be conniving egotists who will stab me in the back out of greed for more luxury and money."

Those were Elvis's words—three weeks before he died.

23. The Buzzards Picking Elvis's Dead Flesh

Elvis Presley's body hadn't been buried before the buzzards—insensitive, inhuman opportunists—were concocting nefarious schemes to use Elvis's death as a moneymaker! *"Anything to make a fast buck."* Many of them had already frantically rushed such devious plans into operation. It was like a holocaust of never-ending, money-grabbing carnival-honky-tonk twiddle-twaddle—and it did enrich the pockets and bank accounts of innumerable vultures.

Thousands of people were pouring into Memphis to pay their last respects to their idol. Scalpers bought up hundreds of editions of the Memphis newspapers publishing accounts of Elvis's death, funeral plans and what was going on in the city. They hawked them as souvenirs, and grief-stricken fans paid as much as $25 to $100 a copy. Some of the entrepreneurs gleefully reported they had been able to buy brand-new Cadillacs with the profit. Others claimed,

"I made $10,000 profit which will put my child through college."

Two days after Elvis's demise, hawkers had Elvis emblazoned T-shirts for sale, Elvis Presley Boulevard signs, and all kinds of handkerchiefs, shirts, and ties "selling like hotcakes right here in Memphis." And right across the street from Graceland.

The hardcover edition of the book Elvis and I worked on for eighteen years, which was published by Drake in 1975, had long been sold out before Elvis's passing. Overnight, collector-fans were offering $100 a copy and searching in bookstores throughout the country for remaining copies. Some even put ads in movie fan journals in the hope of securing a copy. Such was the extent of the "Elvis Mania"—and not all of it was an attempt to make money off of his dead flesh. Many of Elvis's most loyal admirers wished only to secure a treasured memory, something he had approved of while he was alive.

Alas that what was true of the buyers was so far from true for the sellers of Elvis memorabilia. Within days, big advertisements appeared in the national press media, advertising "Elvis Presley home movies, informal close-ups taken at home, off guard. See his intimate, personal life—in the shower, with Priscilla, his mother, his daughter Lisa Marie" . . . on and on. The films started selling at $20 a hundred feet and soon were up to $1000. Elvis's own home movies? Elvis never posed for any home movies for a professional photographer, but he had plenty of home movies.

What were they really like?

Elvis was so careful to guard the privacy of his personal life that he had his own camera record his parties, holiday celebrations, and all of the birthdays of little Lisa Marie. One special Beverly Hills camera store was entrusted to develop and make the prints. When a picture of Elvis and Priscilla and Lisa Marie appeared on the cover of a movie magazine, Elvis was furious. He had been "sold out" by someone in the store. Who? All denied it, of course, but there was the picture! Tracking it down, he discovered an extra print had been made and sold to a movie magazine for $3,700! Elvis immediately built his own darkroom at home. He developed and printed his own pictures. So where did these nefarious, widely advertised Elvis home movies come from. We may never know.

Meanwhile, early in September 1977, Elvis pictures on buttons were selling by the thousands. A wire-service photographer asked permission to use a head shot of Elvis and me for a button. "They'll sell like anything, make me a lot of money," he said. "Besides, that's a cute picture of you and Elvis."

"If you do," I replied coldly, "I'll sue you! To me, that would be the most tasteless thing I can imagine." Others close to Elvis were not so reticent.

Elvis Figures were put on the market—cheap plaster of paris for $25, stone for $100. Some had Elvis swinging his hips. Others had him playing his guitar. None actually looked like Elvis. Fans protested about these cheap, paltry-looking imitations which were coming out by thousands. Elvis had dignity and class, they cried. Why cheapen his memory? That was the message in hundreds of cards and letters I received. Thousands more must have reached Graceland.

Before Elvis's death there were some 176 Elvis imitators, singing his songs and dressing like Elvis. All over the world, they were trying to be carbon copies of Elvis Presley. None of course possessed Elvis's charisma, his magic, his electric excitement, no matter how much they tried. Many of these inpersonators had played Las Vegas while Elvis was still alive and had tried to reach him. Elvis simply shrugged his shoulders. He could have legally stopped them. But Elvis, with his typical generosity, let them go. These "would-be's" never got and never will get the cool $250,000 a week that was the genuine, real Elvis Presley's salary. And so they twanged away on their cheap guitars, advertising their antics as "A Tribute To Elvis." *Tribute?* Or is it just for the money? Whichever it was, one thing is for sure. No one ever challenged their right to mimic Elvis until several months after Elvis's death!

Imitation is said to be the sincerest form of flattery, but apparently Elvis Presley's song publishers, who took legal steps to limit the theatrical use of Presley material, don't believe in this famous old saying. Imitators now must obtain specific contract approval. Expensive? Yes. But obviously worth it.

Until recently, Colonel Parker had considered the imitators "small potatoes." After Elvis's death, more and more Elvis imitators sprang up in all parts of the world. All were trying to look, sound, and dress like Elvis and all used his songs and material.

Broadcast Music Inc. notified performers and theater owners that strict statutes limited the use of Presley songs. BMI, one of the major song-licensing agencies and the representative of various publishers who were desirous of protecting the rights to their Presley tunes, took action! While singers can still use Presley songs in concert or nightclub acts, they must first secure dramatic and grant rights from each publisher if they use more than three of that publisher's songs. It is known that the producers of *Beatlemania*, a smash success on Broadway, had to first secure such performance rights to the John Lennon–Paul McCartney songs before they could mount their production.

Otherwise, the show couldn't have opened. In a year the show generated hundreds of thousands of dollars for the music publishers. And obtaining such rights is costly!

Managers of Elvis imitators, now aware of the limits imposed on their would-be Elvises, had to come to legal terms—or else! The only generous publisher seemed to be Sam Phillips of Sun Records, who had released Elvis's first singles. He initially intimated, but may have changed his mind, that he wouldn't stop anyone from singing his company's Hi Lo tunes, "Blue Suede Shoes" and "Mystery Train." Screen Gems owns the rights to "Suspicious Minds", Tree owns "Heartbreak Hotel", and Combine owns "Burning Love." The Gladys and Elvis Presley Music Co. and Hudson, Leiber and Stoller Co. own dozens of Presley songs including "Hound Dog," "Don't Be Cruel," "Can't Help Falling in Love," "Love Me Tender," "Teddy Bear," and "I Want You, I Need You, I Love You." Many of Elvis's greatest later hits belonged to other tunesmiths and publishers.

On the heels of Elvis's death, the number of Elvis Presley imitators rose to 219—many of whom were asking and getting big salaries on the nightclub circuit. Some invited me to see their shows to convince me they were Elvis reincarnated. Two in Las Vegas played to sold-out houses; they were obviously the best of the imitators judging from the salaries they demanded. Peddling their brand of nostalgia, they played to capacity crowds. Their frequently uttered justification for their, to say the least, lucrative doings is: "We are doing this only to keep the memory of Elvis alive."

Some of the more daring Elvis impersonations, I am told, even made use of billboards covered with blowups of the genuine Elvis performing but announcing the name of a pale copy. Again, Elvis's image was being used as "the come-on," merely to make money, by exploiting the beloved memory of the King of Rock 'n' Roll.

With RCA printing Elvis records on a twenty-four-hour-a-day schedule in an attempt to keep up with the immediate demands created by his death, and with Elvis himself having sold 500 million records during his lifetime—and another estimated million in the few days following his demise—it is logical to assume that the world did not need any imitations of Elvis to keep his memory alive. If the legend of Valentino, whose legacy is a mere handful of movies, unassisted by either records or TV, could still be so very much alive fifty years after his demise—with new books and movies, the latest in 1977, about his life still being made—then Elvis, with thirty-two motion pictures, several television specials, countless personal appearances, concert tours, and some 600 million records, can hardly be in danger of being forgotten. No, Elvis can certainly stand on his own.

Amazing was the lack of gentility, honest feelings, and respect that was expressed by some writers in the tacky articles they wrote, belittling all Elvis stood for to millions of people the world over. Their impressions of Elvis Presley were 100 percent in conflict with the letters (3600 at that point, and still coming in fast) I had received from Elvis's friends and fans who had "put their money where their mouths are," by buying Elvis records, attending his concerts, and seeing his films and TV specials.

Here is a taste of a typical article, written by a teacher of English in California. The title of his piece read: "All Hail the Satanic King of Sneer. It Was Elvis Who Drove Me to the Gates of Eternal Damnation." To summarize, the writer mentioned

everything about Elvis—his hair, his sneer, his daring
pelvic maneuvers, his music itself—and ran down the
list of all those horrified parents, school officials, cler-
gymen, and other self-proclaimed guardians of clean
living and morality.

What this writer failed to understand was that Elvis
had an overwhelming physical presence that was perfectly suited to his physical music. And if the writer is
upset by what he calls Elvis's sneer, he should be re-
minded of the fact that Elvis had plenty to sneer
about, and perhaps his grandest sneer of all was to
flaunt his newly won wealth with a vengeance. This is
something middle-class liberals and middle-class
leftists can't readily comprehend. They want their
heroes to be austere and self-abnegating, to practice
the cult of lowered expectations, and they can't stand
anything like Elvis's or Ali's Cadillacs.

Furthermore, I doubt whether any of these refined
souls ever told Elvis to his face that his display of
wealth was so "vulgar." Had the writer of that article
met Elvis in person, he would never have drawn such
a scathing portrait, because he would have seen that
the real Elvis was nothing like the picture he painted
at all.

Another comment that was brought to my attention can be found in Harriet Van Horne's column of
September 12, 1977. Its title reads: *"Not Very Smart,
Either;* America, Judging by Its Heroes, *Is Tacky."* In
part, she wrote: "Some people say it's drink and
drugs. Others speak of our intellectual sloth, the new
illiteracy and the rip-off spirit that holds nothing
sacred. They certainly qualify as sick, all those sorry
states. Elvis Presley is a melancholy example. He had,
in his prime, a certain animal vitality. Not talent, not
charm, just screaming, stomping energy. He died a
fat, pill-using, poorly educated man. He had a face-

lift before forty, never learned to play more than the 'open positions' on the guitar, and is remembered by his intimates for his vanity, abusive temper, and occasional bursts of generosity."

All I can say to Ms. Van Horne is that if she had only known Elvis in person—Elvis, who had only to read a page of script twice and it was committed to memory, one of the most photographic memories, say film directors, ever known; who never flubbed his lines before the camera in the thirty-two pictures he made; who was judged by the musicians who recorded with him as "a very fine musician"; who worked on his own arrangements and songs and who, besides playing the guitar, played the piano by ear and could accompany and entertain you for hours. Elvis never had a music lesson; his talent was God-given. Elvis became highly educated by reading books—endless reading of all kinds: philosophy, history, biographies, religion, government, etc. He had an intellectual mind. He had a wonderfully warm, magnetic personality. He never was known to say an unkind word to or about anyone, but was known for his unusually good manners and politeness. In no way, for any amount of headlines, money or notoriety, achieved by some who've taken it upon themselves to write scathing, untruthful articles about him, would Elvis have done likewise. "Meanness" was no part of his nature. Had he been the slightest measure otherwise, millions of people would not have so loved him.

Elvis's exciting, personal charisma gave him the greatest career the entertainment world has ever known.

Some so-called fans, alas, even got into the "Make Money on Elvis's Death" racket. Some offered a flower from his grave for $10 per . . . and bought the flowers from florists. Heartbroken Elvis fans paid

as much as $25 for these bogus blooms. Some of El-
vis's "best" false friends offered clothing Elvis had
given to them—and other gifts including radios, even
jewelry—for big money. Nothing is sacred, evidently,
to people who want to make "a fast buck off the
dead." Is this cannibalistic?

Inquiring reporters, visiting Memphis and anxious
for true Elvis stories, sought Elvis's relations.

Elvis never discussed his many relatives—the many
Presleys, who are scattered throughout the South, and
the many Smiths on his mother Gladys's side. Elvis
had often helped the industrious and the well mean-
ing of his very large family. But he had no pity for
the "bummers" who would have liked to live off his
hard work and earnings—the easy way.

If any relation was ever hard hit by some trend in
the national economy or helplessly caught in a wave
of unemployment—without a job and being downright very poor, Elvis could never turn him down. Yet
there were many who felt they should have had far
more attention and money than they received. Some
often remarked openly that "if Gladys, Elvis's mother,
were alive, she'd be helping and sharing with us. But
after she died, a lot of the good things were cut off."

While Elvis was alive, the Smiths and the Presleys
in the majority lined their walls with newspaper press
clippings and photographs of Elvis. Knowing his dislike of them talking about him to the press, most of
them remained very closemouthed. Many of the press
had previously journeyed to Tennessee and Mississippi, making inquiries, trying to obtain factual
material on Elvis from the relatives. And without
success.

When Elvis died, however, "scarcely before poor,
dear Elvis was cold, and not even in his grave yet,"

many of his kin were calling the press offering all kinds of stories on Elvis. Naturally for money. Elvis would never have believed they could have turned his love and care for them so quickly aside—for pure greed.

Perhaps the most flagrant news that some of Elvis's relatives whipped out to the press was an old prison record on Vernon Presley. This disclosure was given out purely for money.

It is well known that Gladys and Vernon Presley were extremely poor when they married. Elvis often remarked to me: "You can't know how my parents suffered, just to get enough for us to eat. Mama's big worry always was that some sickness would come and we wouldn't have the money for medicine, or even a doctor, or to go to the hospital, if it was a matter of saving a life. It was at Mama's insistence, to be near a hospital, that we moved from Tupelo to Memphis when I was a little boy. Mama scrubbed floors in a hospital,"

According to certain of Elvis's relatives, Vernon did time in prison when Elvis was three years old. Vernon was having a hard time feeding his own family and went, in a dire emergency, to the aid of his brother-in-law, who was even worse off. The men worked for only six or seven dollars a week on farms. It is said that Gladys's brother Travis, who years later became a security guard at Graceland, was desperately in need of help, and that together with Vernon and a third person, they were ultimately found guilty of forging a check of a little over $100 and sent to jail. It is said they were shackled and worked on chain gangs where they were bullwhipped by vicious guards. Some of the welts left hideous scars on the men's backs. Mrs. Orsen Bean, whose late husband was the forgery victim, refused to discuss the matter out of respect for the Presleys. But the transcript from the Circuit Court Minute Book No. 13, for the May 5, 1938, court hearing records the document that sent Vernon to jail. Why would anyone dig up the misdeed of a very young man, which Vernon was at the time, except for greed? Vernon was never an evil man.

Other relatives gave writers all kinds of stories and tried to dig up scandal or whatever else they could imagine to say about Elvis for books. Most of it was untrue.

Here again, Elvis was being swindled.

24. Friends Lament Elvis's Memory Turned into a Huckster's Carnival

Elvis was surrounded by many vultures, as well as by people who really cared, respected what he stood for, and loved him for himself. But there were the eager beavers who didn't care about Elvis, but only for the money they got from him, and any fast buck they could make due to their proximity to him, they made. It was very sad. Small wonder that Elvis, near the end of his life, wondered *who* he could trust.

I can still see him saying the words, his face a picture of sadness as he spoke his feelings of betrayal. "It's terrible not knowing who I can trust. The boys work for me, I believed absolutely, on a stack of Bibles if necessary. Everyone has to have someone—someone close you can relax and confide in—can trust—can express your opinions to privately. This is a sacred trust . . . and one I have never broken. No matter, a few people have done me wrong." Elvis grinned at that. "I sound like Mae West," he added, amused at the witticism she had coined and he was using. "I never reveal who. But I never trust them again.

"Sometimes my daddy has told me, 'You can't trust—this one! He did that wrong to you!' If it is only minor, I call that person to me and we discuss it. Then we wipe the slate clean and we start all over again. Jesus taught all of us that.

"I can be furious at the moment for any injustice, believe me. I let the sparks fly. It gets plenty hot for a few minutes. But I don't hold grudges. Even when I have fired one of the boys working for me . . . when they come to me again with the plea they are broke and they need money for their wife or kid, I always take them back.

"I'm told this is being too soft. But when I understand the circumstances and the needs, I justify. I'm not a softie, and I don't stay fooled for very long."

Another fan, a young man, called me long distance from Denver: "I am disgusted," he said, "with all of the cheap stuff they are palming off on Elvis Presley, who was a great personality and a super big star. It's like his death is an overnight circus, with all the trashy sideshow tricks and mementos, even cheap, cotton-stuffed Elvis dolls, plaster-of-paris terrible likenesses of Elvis, license plates—any kind of junk they can figure to make a fast buck on a dead star. I resent it. Elvis is gone. Why isn't there some respect for his memory? There was nothing cheap about Elvis. He was the King. The way he is being treated as a disgrace!"

Then came a long distance call from Memphis and these words: "It is interesting to see Elvis's purple Cadillac on display here on Elvis Presley Boulevard.

It is a gold-plate 1956 Eldorado convertible, owned by a car dealer here who paid less than $1000 for it when Elvis traded it in on a new car years ago. The car dealer has it in mint condition and values it today at a million dollars. You can look at it for free. He also has a guitar Elvis gave him, he says, in 1975, on display. Seems they were on together in music when Elvis used to cut for Sun Records in the beginning of his career. The car is a worthy tribute to the King."

And long distance from South Dakota came these words: "I was lucky to be able to enter Graceland on Elvis's birthday and see his grave. It is a beautiful sight. There were so many floral offerings, from very expensive ones to many a single flower tied with satin bows. Some were shaped like his guitar. Most of them were roses and carnations. A light snow and raindrops kept falling—like tears from heaven on his beautiful grave. My husband and I stood in line for six hours to get in. It was more than well worth it.

"We heard there were Elvis exhibits at the Convention Center and the fairgrounds. We saw a bed Elvis had owned years ago and loved. Everyone wanted to sit on it. An old-fashioned, homemade quilt his grandma had made him was on the bed, with one of his guitars and pictures of him. I met and talked to many other Elvis fans. Some had pieces of him actually, like a piece of his clothing. I had the best—I had a single strand of Elvis's beautiful, black hair in a locket. I treasure this beyond anything in the world except my husband, who understands my love for Elvis and shares it. Some of the fans offered me as much as $150 to buy it. Even $1000 wouldn't tempt me. How did I get it? A relative of mine used to cut Elvis's hair. He always saved the clippings and sells them at $10 an inch length, to $50 for a three-inch length. He has been able to buy himself a new car with the money selling Elvis's hair cuttings."

A long-distance caller from Chicago, Illinois, said: "We are getting up a petition to send to President Carter to declare Elvis's birthday a national holiday. We already have close to 400,000 signers including the Japanese and British who came over by the hundreds in chartered planes to celebrate Elvis's birthday at his grave site at Graceland. How many signatures can you get in Los Angeles, May, for our petition?"

I received a snapshot of a bench which sits opposite the Music Gate at Graceland on Elvis Presley Boulevard. In big letters is painted, "Elvis." In smaller letters, "In Memory of January 8, 1935, August 16, 1977. Lansky." It is there for those too sick, too old, or too weary to stand during the long waits to enter Graceland.

There came many long-distance calls from Elvis fans who do not approve of all the imitators of Elvis on stages all over the world. "Some even have had plastic surgery to try to look like Elvis," some said. "No one can look like Elvis, nor have his magnetic charm, marvelous winning smile, and electrifying personality. These fast-buck imitators are not paying him any needed tribute. They are just out for the hard, cold cash," said one man calling from New York City. Many calls came on the announcement that a movie was to be made of Elvis's life. All of them were protests. Elvis is scarcely gone—and who could possibly portray him on the screen? Most fans resented it this soon, or at least this was the jist of the letters I received, many of them from fan club prexies. Again, it was all to make money on Elvis. Personally, I had several movie queries on my book, *The Private Elvis*, one from a man who was tall and attractive and did look somewhat like Elvis, except he couldn't sing. It was his goal to make an Elvis movie, and he considered Elvis to be in the public domain. He kept calling and asking me questions: "What was Elvis really like?" etc., etc.—a big waste of my time. I personally think that making a film on Elvis when he was not even dead a year was in very bad taste and was certainly not a brilliant idea. Elvis's death was still too new, too fresh in everyone's mind and heart. We can see Elvis on TV specials, in the thirty-two movies he left behind, and play his records to relive Elvis Presley. Who wants an imitation Elvis show? Perhaps as time goes on we may come to feel otherwise, but for now . . .

"It's like buzzards," a friend in Memphis, who knew Elvis and his family well, called to tell me. "Everyone who can think of some ridiculous claim to put in on Elvis's estate is trying everything she or he can think of to do it." Some are crackpots. Some were even close to Elvis. One said Elvis had promised him $5000 in his will! Another claimed Elvis had hurt him with a karate chop six years ago in a practice in Los Angeles. A show girl in Las Vegas claimed Elvis had promised her a Cadillac, and where is it?

So many want a piece of Elvis. Now he's gone, and they are greedily suing for his money!

Next, Elvis's luxurious home, sitting on a mountaintop in Palm Springs, was advertised for sale. The price: $450,000. In spite of special police patrols, thieves broke in. They crashed the glass of a louvered window. Lights flooded the house, inside and outside, and alarm bells began ringing. The thieves hastily departed on the run, before police arrived.

Elvis had built the house according to his own plans in 1965. Set on two acres of beautifully landscaped acreage, it has fifteen rooms, a Jacuzzi, sauna, steam room, swimming pool and a large, elaborate playroom complete with bars.

The house, inherited by Lisa Marie in Elvis's will, was offered "for sale" along with its lavish furnishings—all of which had been personally selected by Elvis.

25. Love Letters for Elvis to Me

These are excerpts of letters from those who love Elvis, from the many thousands who have written and sent them to me, some five thousand since Elvis died, and from all parts of the world. It was difficult to select only a few, for they are all very worthwhile and heartwarming. It is not possible for me to reply to the thousands of letters . . . and I want so much to do so. . . . I hope that this book will serve to acknowledge hearing from all of you and express my heartfelt appreciation for your taking the time to write to me. Elvis, I am sure, is most pleased. Due to the constraints of space, the following were picked at random.

"Dear Miss Mann: I would like to say that I thoroughly enjoyed your book, *The Private Elvis*. I don't like to read very much but I read your book in four days, which for me is good. I'm so glad you knew Elvis as a real person. I wish I could have met Elvis. I did get a chance to see him here in Detroit at the

Olympia Stadium back in 1970. I bought some pictures of him.

"The one big picture is now on my front-room wall in a frame. I am thirty-seven years of age with four children. Elvis had always been my idol and always will be forever. Your book was warm and written with lots of feeling. I enjoyed every minute of it. I have a lot of Elvis's albums, singles, and the one with the piece of his clothing and the large full pictures of Elvis. I taped his last concert—which I wish they had never put on TV. His eyes looked so bad, so ill—I was heartsick. This man imitator, who has had plastic surgery to try to be Elvis, has a lot of nerve. He'll never, never take Elvis's place. I just cried when I saw his picture next to Elvis's. That man has no right to do what he is doing. Thank you again for such a warm and true book on Elvis. I'm sick of these people who are all trying to make money on Elvis's death. They are so crude and mean. I'm sorry, but Elvis was too good of a person to have other people make a fortune off him. I hope you will write about Elvis again. Thank you for such a beautiful, true book, which Elvis helped you write before he died. Sincerely, N.K., Taylor, Michigan, March 1978."

Schiller wrote that "Man is an imitative creature, and whoever is foremost leads the heart and the herd." Willmott said that "We imitate only what we believe and admire," and Goethe that "Men are so constituted that every one undertakes what he sees another successful in, whether he has the aptitude for it or not." Finally, South wrote that "Every kind of imitation speaks the person that imitates inferior to him whom he imitates, as the copy is to the original."

Elvis will always stand head and shoulders above any imitators. The Beatles, Tom Jones, the Rolling

Stones are perhaps the only enduring ones. They all acknowledge the King, the creator of rock 'n' roll, the music which gave them careers.

"I am a student at the Ulan Ude Agriculture College here in Ulan Ude. I am also a Buryat, who worked in the Lenin Collective Farm in Trukhoy. We heard an Elvis recording at secret gatherings in town. A visitor from your country, America, brought your book on Elvis Presley here. I can't tell you how excited and happy we are to have it. We pass it around to close friends. We pray, now that a couple of hundred other students have been able to read it, that it will not fall apart. If anyone you know is coming here, please, I beg you, send us some more of your Elvis books. Sincerely, A.B., Ulan Ude."

"Congratulations for writing a real, large-as-life book on our idol Elvis. I attended Harvard University. There were many of us Japanese in Boston who were and are Elvis fans. Your books are all over in the stores here in Tokyo and Nagoya. They sell as fast as they get them. Will you be doing another book to tell us what really happened to Elvis since your other one was written, I believe, in 1975? T.O., Nagoya, Japan."

"How I love Elvis, loved him, love him. Here in Italy when he died, the radios all day played his music, and our TV went into mourning. I cried and cried. On a visit to my relatives earlier last year in Brooklyn, New York, they told me Elvis was appearing nearby in concert, and they took me. It was the highlight of my life. By a devious plan, since one of my relatives had the popcorn concession at the auditorium, I got backstage. As Elvis was walking out to his car I got him to sign your book. I'll bet *you* don't even have such a treasure. He signed it, 'To R——, Best Wishes, Elvis.' R.P., Milan, Italy."

"I am an old fan of Elvis's. I am fifty-two years old, a grandma eight times. Elvis was the greatest singer, the most handsome man—everything about him was to be admired. I can't get over his death. I still sit and cry. I have four daughters. One of them, Linda, saw him in person. She is expecting a baby and will name him Elvis if the baby is a boy. God bless you for sharing Elvis for real with us. Mrs. J.B., Wilmo, Virginia."

"Thank you, May, for saying the true nice things about someone who was a part of my life and millions more. L.D., Green Bay, Wisconsin."

"My heart is so full of things I want to say. I always enjoyed Elvis as a performer, but that's always the way he remained in my heart, because I was never able to know him as a real person. Your book thrilled me so, for now he has become much more to me. Your book made me realize he was truly more wonderful than I ever began to realize. He was really an open, warm, and loving man who cared about people. Other stars never seem interested in us. They remain untouched and distant. But not our Elvis. I see now he started out caring and never quit. Through you, he has become real, and in a sense I feel I've touched him and know him in a way I never thought possible.

"It has bothered me to read other books on Elvis where the authors made him seem crude, impersonal, and cold. Your book opened a window and let in the fresh air and sunshine. It's nice to know he wasn't a disappointment in any way. Thanks for caring about him and us enough to write the real, honest truth and not lies. I am sure you were a ray of sunshine to him, in his last, troubled days. For he had only to read your book. C.T., Aurora, Colorado."

"It is now four days since I was hit by the shocking news of Elvis Presley's death. I still feel it, like the loss of a brother. I've been an Elvis fan for over twenty years, and followed his career. The press here has been filled with all kinds of news for four days and even on handbills. And look, with Elvis dead, they have now changed all the terrible, rotten stuff they were printing and are now praising Elvis. Our biggest stores here are selling your hardcover *Elvis*, as well as the paperback, and everyone's buying them as fast as they come in. Thank you for being a real friend to Elvis. J.W., Gothenburg, Sweden."

"I enjoyed your closeness to Elvis very much and envy your spending so much time with him. I have been a fan of his for nine years. Now I am at the ripe old age of sixteen years old. I have his records and have my room covered in posters and pictures. Of course in Britain you don't get enough of Elvis. The saddest day of my life was 16th August 1977. I don't know how you took the news but you have my deepest sympathy along with millions of other fans just like myself.

"I was walking down our busy road near my house. I was going to the chip shop. I got my chips and walked along with my boyfriend, and we were telling jokes and laughing. At the corner my dad was waiting. I knew something was wrong, and he said that he was just out for a walk. He pulled my boyfriend over and whispered in his ear, then he came over and said that he was just telling him that he liked his haircut. Then I heard my boyfriend say to my dad, 'You're kidding me on.' My boyfriend went over to his own house and my dad walked me home. . . . My dad said, 'Linda, I have some bad news for you.' I said, 'What is it?' My dad said, 'Your best friend has died.' I thought he meant my best girl friend, and I said, 'Mary?' He said, 'No—Elvis has just died.'

"My face went white. I felt very pale. I told my dad never to joke like that again, that it wasn't something to joke about, but he said it was true. Then I believed him. I started to cry; the tears rolled down my cheeks, I thought my world had come apart. Someone I hadn't met had died and now there was emptiness, but I thought of Elvis as a very dear friend and companion. I grew up listening to Elvis and he was part of my day-to-day life. When I felt depressed I played some of his records and I would be happy again. When I thought I was putting on weight I would play 'Jailhouse Rock' and dance the fastest rock 'n' roll dance, and in a few weeks the fatness would disappear. Elvis helped me in a lot of ways.

"My sister, who is fourteen years old, was being comforted by my mum, who also is an Elvis fan. Her eyes were swollen and red with crying, but by this time my tears had stopped. Then a news flash came over the television. It showed a picture of Elvis taken when he was thirty-four years old, wearing a blue jump suit. My memory blanked as I let out a scream. Then my neighbors all came down when they heard the news. An hour later when I had calmed down a little bit, my dad told me he came down to meet me to make sure I was all right, because he thought I may have heard the news flash on the television in the chip shop. He also thought that if I had heard it, I might have done something stupid. Who knows?

"The first news flash was very stupid. The announcer came on the air and said Elvis was dead! Then he got a phone call and said, 'Wait a minute, Elvis is still alive and has been rushed to the hospital.' Catastrophe could have happened if he didn't come on the air and say for definite whether Elvis was dead or alive. Ten minutes later the news flash came that Elvis had just died in the hospital. It was all too much for me. I decided to go to bed and sleep it off.

"After a very disturbing night's rest, I couldn't face going to work in the morning, so I stayed off. Everything was a nightmare. I put on the radio and all day long you could hear Elvis records and announcements saying, 'The King of Rock 'n' Roll is dead.' I fought the tears as I watched the one o'clock news. They were displaying Elvis's life story and clippings from pictures. One clipping was from a programme which Britain never managed to see. Elvis was singing 'It's Over.' He looked so healthy, so handsome. Then it showed outside his mansion in Memphis, and the crowds gathering to pay their last respects. The morning paper showed a full spread photo of Elvis in Hawaii and the headline, 'Elvis Dead.' That night one TV station put on 'Elvis—That's the Way It Is'—fantastic. But I still couldn't accept Elvis's death.

"I was horrified about two weeks later when Elvis hit the headlines again. It was in the *Daily Record* published in Glasgow. The headline was 'Elvis,' then a subheading. 'His Last Photograph from His Memphis Mansion.' It was a photo of Elvis lying peacefully in his coffin. It caused a lot of gossip and comments. It made me sick. I kept asking why did they have to show Elvis, they don't do that to anybody else. Since his death I have collected all the papers with Elvis in them, all the tribute magazines and a lot of his records, especially his Number 1 hit, 'Way Down' and also the fan club tribute record, 'I Remember Elvis Presley.' My favorite Elvis record is 'The Wonder of You,' which I haven't got because it is very hard to get here in Britain. To me Elvis will never die and to many other fans. We will always be true to the King. *Long live the music of the late King Elvis Presley.* Elvisly yours, L.H., Glasgow, Scotland, Great Britain."

"As I was growing up, my dad wouldn't let me go to see Elvis. Then I got married and my husband was the same. I have all Elvis's records and posters and have read everything you've been writing about him, and seeing your pictures with him over the years. Now since his death, my husband has apologized to me for not taking me to one of Elvis's concerts. He's promised to take me to Graceland this year. There was no special age group that adored Elvis, for my mother is fifty-seven, and she's one of his most devoted fans. My husband now understands my feeling and he tried to comfort me during Elvis's funeral, and for days after all those reports on Elvis's death. K.M., Shelby, North Carolina."

"My friends warned me that any book out on Elvis was just paste-up jobs from any source with some photos and not to waste my money. Finally I found your book, and I couldn't lay it down. It was the best book ever written on Elvis. I then saw you had written a book on Jayne Mansfield. I couldn't lay it down either and read it right through. Then I got the movie, 'The Girl Can't Help It,' on video tape, and I now have a different view on both stars. Thank you millions. S.L., Sweden."

"The world has suffered a great loss in the sudden death of Elvis Presley, but with the true cooperation of 'May Mann's book,' it helps the fan and book readers to understand Elvis for real. I love you too for writing it. I am twenty-one years of age. V.H., Glasgow, Scotland."

"I saw Elvis in concert in Syracuse, New York, in July, and he was energetic, sexy, and loving. When he sang, 'You Gave Me a Mountain,' you knew he felt it and he meant it with all of his heart and soul. It made me cry for him. I hope you write more on Elvis and give those stupid villains the putdown they deserve. B.R., Elmira, New York."

"All those stupid, vicious stories about Elvis, orgies, and drugs . . . I can't bring myself to read more than the first few pages of such crap about a world idol. I read your *Elvis and the Colonel* and *The Private Elvis* over and over and over, and I get something new about Elvis that is so endearing each time. He must have loved you very, very much to help you write such a real book showing him as a human being and a loving, caring man for his fellow men. I'm making a pilgrimage to Graceland and am saving all of my earnings to make it. Just to pick a blade of grass for a keepsake from Graceland will be worth the scrimping to do it.

"Elvis was such a special part of all of our lives. We all hurt when his mom died. It was like we'd lost part of our own family. We just wanted to hold him and say, 'Cry it out and it will hurt less someday.'

When he and Priscilla divorced, we prayed they'd get back together if that would make him happy. And poor little Lisa Marie. When he was sick or depressed, we'd pray he'd be better soon. S.E., Ithaca, New York."

"I have only become an Elvis fan in recent years. You portray Elvis as I hear him on records. I can never understand how I could hear one person and see him on TV, and read about someone so entirely different. He sings as a tender, caring, and lonesome man. We saw him perform at Pontiac Stadium New Year's Eve, from the sixth row. I had the feeling he wasn't well and was having a difficult time expending the energy he felt necessary. How unselfish he was to come out and do his best not to disappoint his fans. You have renewed my belief in all he was. J.W., Marine City, Michigan."

"I have been in love with Elvis since I was fourteen, bought all his records, and enjoyed his films and music. I always felt he was a good human being. I never believed he was into drugs and aloof. And I did not really realize how he felt about people and how friendly and sincere he was to everyone, until I read your book. He was more down-to-earth than most people. I know now he had a tender heart. When the news came of his death, I could hardly believe it. I had heard rumors about his being ill and his weight problem the last two years. He was so young and so talented and cared so much for people.

"All those bad pictures painted of him I have disbelieved. He didn't change from a well-mannered, loving, warm human being that your book reaffirms. He gave so much to everyone, I wonder what we can give back to him. I saw him on stage February 14,

1977 at St. Petersburg, Florida. I had waited twenty years to see him. I wanted him to sing on forever. I wanted one of those scarves. I wanted to say, 'Hi,' and meet him. I felt as high as a kite just from being there, listening to him.

"I ask, like everyone else, 'Why did Elvis have to die so young?' I take comfort that he is with Our Lord and God and at peace. While I was just one more fan, who never met him and he never knew I existed, I feel I have lost a dear, dear friend. He was many things to each of us. Thank you for your book on Elvis. This is the first fan letter I've ever written. We all love you for it. C.R., Pinellas Park, Florida."

"I wish I could never have finished your book—I want to read more. I grew up with Elvis. I am twenty-three years old, have three children, and ever since I can remember I loved his voice. Whenever I hear his songs, I feel just as you did, that he was talking to me. I now knew the real man from your writings. I cry as I sit here writing to you, for this wonderful man who had so many material things, but was lonely in so many ways. I can see how much you cared for him, and I'm sure he loved you very much the same way. I had written to him at Graceland, telling him not to work so hard, to get well. I told him if he ever wanted to get away from the rat race to come to our beautiful home here, for a rest. No one would bother him. We could give him a beautiful cabin. And he could bring his Lisa Marie. I almost envy you being his friend. The only way I can be his friend, and he mine, is through your beautiful, loving book.

"If you visit his grave, please put a wild flower on it for me. I am sure he was very proud of the book when it first came out. By it, Elvis is no longer a voice on records to me. He will always be the wonderful, warm, loving man you told me of in your book. I know he must have meant so much to you, and I also feel he must have known he had a very good and wonderful friend in you. J.B., Sioux Lookout, Ontario, Canada."

"I can appreciate the fact that Priscilla wanted to do her own thing. You wrote beautifully of her. But she should have done that before she married Elvis. Her life, after her marriage, should have been completely devoted to him, as his wife. Millions of girls and women would have given anything for that chance. B.S., San Francisco, California."

"Thank you for caring for Elvis and by you, we millions of fans have a beautiful way to remember a very gracious, warm, and wonderful human being, and a great, talented singer, as Elvis Aron Presley. I read your book with an aching heart and tears in my eyes. Chapter 30 to the very end really got to me. Every word you wrote said it all. Even though I was sure jealous of you, because of your privileged friendship with Elvis. We all thank you to be able to write it all down and put Elvis in the book form for all of us to read.

"When you think of the people who would come from all over the world to Las Vegas to hear him, it boggles the mind. We attended Elvis's concert June 18, 1977. The man who sold us our tickets gave us lousy treatment, telling my husband and me to hurry up and move on—and after we had stood in line at the ticket booth for hours. Even if we didn't have the best seats for the exorbitant price we paid, we had the pleasure from a great distance of seeing and hearing Elvis and being in the same building. The next day a friend called saying she thought Elvis had been drinking because he didn't act like himself. I said, 'In no way. He's been taking medicines, May Mann has written, for an illness undisclosed.' Another friend said the same. I told them to rush out and get your book and they'd understand. L.M.R., Detroit, Michigan."

"I deeply regret not meeting you, for I saw you walk past the store where I work and I couldn't catch up with you. You were signing autographs, and then you scurried away. I love your book on Elvis. I really loved him with all of my heart. Meeting you would be the closest I would ever come to Elvis himself. With all my respect and admiration for you and Elvis. Long Live the King, Elvis! J.B., Reseda, California."

"I'm not a teenager. I'm as old as Elvis. Do you think you could write a new book to expose the one Elvis's bodyguards wrote? I and millions of Elvis fans, who knew the truth, don't want that book to be the one everyone will connect with Elvis. Mrs. S.B., Des Moines, Iowa."

"If you will please picture this. It's August 16, 1977, and your eighteenth birthday. You wake up feeling like everything is now going your way. You're now that golden age: legal. Friends stop by to celebrate your birthday. Your parents give you an envelope from the Hartford Civic Center. Inside is a $10 ticket to see my all-time favorite, Elvis Presley, in concert. You're overjoyed. And you're more so when friends bring birthday gifts of Elvis's lp's, 'Hound

Dog,' only acquired by mail, and his latest 'Blue Moods.' The perfect birthday for someone who loves Elvis, as if he was her own father. You're listening so happily to your new Elvis lp's, and your mother comes in with the evening paper that headlines, 'The King of Rock 'n' Roll succumbs at Age 42.' I was crushed. I've lost the most important part of my life.

"Why are people trying to kidnap his body? Why are papers publishing such false stories about a world idol, who is an inspiration to millions? Why did they put a picture of him in his coffin in the papers? I can't stand all of this. Don't they know they are crucifying all of his family and his fans, but most of all little Lisa Marie, who is so innocent? Your book was a salvation. The pictures in it show his mom was very beautiful. And as Elvis got older he started to look like his father. I'd like to write to Priscilla to convey my sympathy too. S.S., Springfield, Massachusetts."

"I wish Elvis could have taken time to see the world and enjoyed himself. Elvis had so much to give; his beautiful smile, his great heart in song. I know Elvis was always thinking what he could do for everyone else and his family. He left them all well off but his little girl really needs him. He did give her so much love, she will always feel him near her. May, you have always, through all of Elvis's career, been a true friend to Elvis. I feel Elvis really treasured you. May God bless you always, May dear, for your beautiful writings about him over many, many years. I am sending your book out to friends as gifts. I wish I could afford to send this beautiful book of a beautiful man, who so lived for his mother, to every Vietnam veteran in the hospitals of America. I wish every true American could read with pride such a heartwarming story of the beautiful, unselfish life of a truly great American. Mrs. M.R., Honolulu, Hawaii."

"It was so great to read the personal, inside life of Elvis in your book. I have had a feeling Elvis was a very ill man. My doctor told me Elvis had had glaucoma and that with some family weakness in his body which he had inherited, it was just a matter of time before he died, and before he went blind. God took him. It was terribly unfair that he had to live such a secluded life. I've visited Graceland, sat on the front steps of his house, and took pictures. I sit many hours thinking of Elvis—such a beautiful soul. I watched his last concert on TV, and it was plain to see how ill he was. Everyone should read your book whether they are a fan or not, to get a better understanding of such a beautiful human being who comes to this world so rarely. He deserves so much credit for his courage to go on, so ill, rather than disappoint his fans. For all he was, and remains, I love him more than ever. What a super person. Mrs. T.H., Auckland, New Zealand."

"Your book was the most truthful, candid book I've ever read. I am fifteen years of age and too young to have known all of this about Elvis. I do hope you write more as there are so many of us younger fans who want to know about the King from his beginning and all. Thanks for writing all to share with us. How unselfish of you. Please write more. J.A., London, England."

"God bless you for writing all about Elvis. Paris and all France went into shock and deep mourning at his death. Please write another book telling us over here what really happened to kill him, what caused him to go out of shape, the truth behind his marriage plans. We are all so curious. Long live Elvis. M.A., Paris, France."

"How we all worshipped Elvis in all Germany. Please write more books on him to tell us of his last years. We love you too for loving Elvis so much. He must have loved you very much to be so confidential with you. He knew he could trust you. A.W., West Berlin, Germany."

26. Epilogue

The allegations that Elvis was on dope caused a furor worldwide, for Elvis was loved, respected, and idolized. His fans are legion, and they are furious, to say the least, that anyone would try to hurt him or diminish his memory.

I know for a fact Elvis would never sniff cocaine or indulge in heroin. He was completely opposed to the drug scene, and he proclaimed this fact from the stage in Las Vegas, for all who were listening to hear. "I've always been an open and honest man," he cried. "I will always continue to be so. I realize writers have to fill their columns and pages with something. But right now I'm setting the record straight." Elvis stood there, defiant, looking straight at his audience of over 2700 people (and a thousand more turned away nightly). *I'm not trying to brag, but I'm an eighth-degree black-belt karate holder. And I'm trying for my ninth and tenth, and I assure you, I'm well able to take care of myself!"*

Elvis was so disturbed by these vicious rumors and so hurt after he learned of the book two of his Mem-

phis Mafia had written, calling him a drug fiend, that
he later referred to his famous onstage outburst in
one of our final hundred-question sessions. "Remember way back how I exploded on stage on my last
show in 1975 in Las Vegas?" he asked.

"I'm quoting exactly what I said then direct from
your book. 'The other night I had the flu that's going
around . . . and real bad. Someone started the
rumor that I was strung out. If I ever find out who
started that, *I'll knock their goddamned head off! I've
never been strung out in my life.*"

The white heat of indignation mellowed as suddenly as it had flared. As he stared out at the
hundreds of shocked and sympathetic faces in the audience, he gave pause, so everyone would know he
was dead serious. "For too long, things are made up
about me. They are all bunk!"

Few people know this, but Elvis actually paid, out
of his very own pocket, to send at least two musicians
to a well-known rehabilitation facility in Connecticut
to kick their habit. I say "at least two" because I
spoke to them myself and I want to stick to fact.
They were so grateful to Elvis.

And what was the upshot of Elvis's generosity?
Someone tried to say that it was Elvis himself who
was in the sanatorium to kick *his* habit!

"I've never been strung out on drugs!" Elvis said,
and he was adamant about this. "Never in my life!"
If Elvis did take medication prescribed by his doctors,
reducing pills to lose weight at strategic times in his
career, and if he did, on occasion, take a pill to relax
from heavy tensions and the pain of his illness—also
prescribed by his doctors—does this mean that Elvis
was on dope?

I doubt that there is one star or starlet, actor or
actress, who at one time or another, in order to lose

weight or to relax from pressures, hasn't had recourse to such prescriptions. Pills, commonly referred to as "uppers," take away the appetite, and "downers" are tranquilizers. It is a common occurrence in show business, where everyone is trying to do his and her best, striving for perfection, and where cameras, as Elvis well knew, add ten to twenty pounds to one's appearance. It has always been the rule to be ten to twenty pounds underweight in order to photograph well. And what star, what glamorous personality in films or television or on the stage, doesn't diet for health and to maintain the physical beauty that is so essential to living a life in the public spotlight?

Liz Smith, the New York columnist, says it well, "The important thing is that Elvis Presley was not, or never was, a dissolute degenerate drug addict." Liz also wrote, "I do ask Elvis lovers, of which I count myself one, to think rationally: if Elvis used uppers and downers, does this really destroy the fine memories of him or his fantastic and unique talent? I think not."

Knowing Elvis as I did and do, I'll never believe he would knowingly take dope. He didn't even like hard liquor. He said he was brought up not to smoke or drink—a common belief he and I shared together in our religion—and one we often discussed. He was known to try to smoke a slim cigar in order to curb his appetite, but he actually hated its taste. Everyone told him it would make dieting easier.

I always remember Elvis saying to me, "Rumors are exaggerated bits of misinformation. I was raised to stand on my own two feet and to make my own decisions. I work hard, and I'll keep on trying, until I work something out. With any fault I may have, if I can pinpoint it, I'll break it . . . or I'll be found dead trying."

Speaking of love Elvis said, "Yes, by nature I am very affectionate, but only with people I like very much. If I should tell a girl, 'I love you,' it would be true. I am sentimental as you well know. I keep souvenirs and love letters, things that are associated with memories. May, I still have the first bicycle my daddy bought me on the weekly payment plan when I was eleven years old. It is up in the attic of Graceland along with all the rest of everything I treasure.

"Loneliness, yes. I have and do know a lot of that. When the fellows are all with their families, like one Christmas Eve, I sat there at Graceland alone. I got on the telephone and called up friends I could think of to wish them a Merry Christmas . . . just to talk to someone . . . just to feel close to someone . . . even if it were only another voice on the telephone. It's funny how often in a big crowd, it hit me for no reason—this inner loneliness. If I start a busy day when I get up . . . everything is fine. If I slow down later, by sundown I always experience deep twinges of loneliness. I like to take a nap at that time, to sleep it away.

"I have found I can't force love. I enjoy being a bachelor, but there is so much more to real living, I well realize, than what I am doing . . . I am long resigned to this way of living, for it is a dedication to a project that the Colonel and I began my career with. But it isn't easy, and I look forward to some day when I'll be free of it all."

Elvis was in a mood to talk that day. "I've done a lot of research on the subject of jealousy and hatred, which I have never experienced personally," he said. "I've talked with ministers and philosophers, after I found out that some of the misinformation on me was

coming out of my own boys for $100 bill handouts.
Jealousy and envy are like cancers eating into your
souls. They can self-destruct and destroy you."

Then his sense of humor took over and he laughed.
"I sound like a preacher. . . . Compulsive hatred,
however, is an emotional sickness full of anguish and
anxiety. It's an under-the-surface power struggle
which can possess the mentality with a resentment
that grows and grows until it destroys all honesty,
honor, and integrity. I've had a lot of time to think
since the first articles appeared, writing that I'm on
dope. I've tried every way to understand why. Then I
got scientific help and I've read up on it, so I know
all about it. I know what I can expect. Some of my
boys thought they were all-important. Some of them
got to beating up people like they were the real law
. . . instead of bodyguards hired to help me get
through the crowds. Luckily, none of the fans got
hurt. It has been a sad awakening for me, that they
could be mean and destructive with just a little au-
thority for keeping the crowds back. Some were suddenly bellowing and hollering Gestapos! I gave them
some strong lectures, man. Told them they could land
in jail if they hurt anyone . . . and I would not defend them. That quieted them down some. But I
sense a lot of repressed, held-in anger in some of
them still. These are the last days and Satan, like the
Bible says, is trying to take over the world before the
millennium comes.

"Look at today—the depravity, the immorality, the
perversions . . . murder, sadism, the debauchery of
things good, the corruption, the cruelty . . . It is
all of this satanic and evil period, the Bible says.

"Well there I go preaching again." Elvis grinned.
"I read the Bible to my men and to my friends. I
have them kneel in prayer with me. Sometimes they

even get tears in their eyes, but their humility is short-lived, I can tell you. I'm not bitter. I keep praying for them. But I do want my friends, my real ones, and my fans, and especially my little daughter, to know the truth of how I feel, how I think. And what I am for real. And I'm arranging that now."

Elvis Presley died alone, so alone, after five hours of terror, unbelievable torture, fear, pain, release, resignation . . . with no one dear or mortal to come to his aid. And then his belief in Jesus took over, and softly and soothingly with grace in his heart, Elvis left us all.

As long as there are his records, his films, as long as there is Graceland and the legend of Elvis Presley, a boy born of the poorest of the poor, uneducated, but with a great gift from God, his music . . . as long as these things live on, his hold on millions of people will not slacken and Elvis will live on for centuries to come.

Elvis's impact on the whole world, the unforgettable sound of his voice, will continue forever. . . .

About the Author

May Mann, a former Miss Utah whose grandfather was one of the presidents of the Mormon Church, is a well-known member of the Hollywood community. For many years a widely syndicated columnist, she continues to write about Hollywood and its personalities in her column "Going Hollywood with May Mann."

Quintessential Quiz Books from SIGNET

(0451)

☐ **THE ELVIS PRESLEY TRIVIA QUIZ BOOK by Helen Rosenbaum.** (081781—$1.50)

☐ **THE SOAP OPERA TRIVIA QUIZ BOOK by Jason Bonderoff.** (117506—$2.75)*

☐ **THE ROLLING STONES TRIVIA QUIZ BOOK by Helen Rosenbaum.** (086694—$1.75)

☐ **THE SUPERHERO MOVIE AND TV TRIVIA QUIZ BOOK by Jeff Rovin.** (084748—$1.75)*

☐ **THE OFFICIAL TV TRIVIA QUIZ BOOK #2 by Bart Andrews.** (084101—$1.50)

☐ **THE NOSTALGIA QUIZ BOOK by Martin A. Gross.** (110358—$2.50)*

☐ **THE OFFICIAL ROCK 'N' ROLL TRIVIA QUIZ BOOK #2 by Marc Sotkin.** (084853—$1.50)

☐ **TREKKIE QUIZ BOOK by Bart Andrews.** (084136—$1.50)

☐ **THE SUPER SIXTIES QUIZ BOOK by Bart Andrews.** (088298—$1.75)*

☐ **FROM THE BLOB TO STAR WARS by Bart Andrews.** (079485—$1.50)

☐ **THE FIRST OFFICIAL NFL TRIVIA QUIZ BOOK by Ted Brock and Jim Campbell.** (095413—$1.95)

☐ **THE SECOND NFL TRIVIA QUIZ BOOK by Jim Campbell.** (117891—$2.25)*

☐ **THE ULTIMATE BASEBALL QUIZ BOOK by Dom Forker.** (096797—$2.50)*

☐ **THE ULTIMATE YANKEE BASEBALL QUIZ BOOK by Dom Forker.** (114299—$2.95)*

☐ **THE ULTIMATE WORLD SERIES QUIZ BOOK by Dom Forker.** (117883—$1.95)*

*Price slightly higher in Canada

Buy them at your local bookstore or use this convenient coupon for ordering.

THE NEW AMERICAN LIBRARY, INC.,
P.O. Box 999, Bergenfield, New Jersey 07621

Please send me the books I have checked above. I am enclosing $_____
(please add $1.00 to this order to cover postage and handling). Send check or money order—no cash or C.O.D.'s. Prices and numbers are subject to change without notice.

Name_____

Address_____

City _____ State . _____ Zip Code _____

Allow 4-6 weeks for delivery.
This offer is subject to withdrawal without notice.